To,

Gill'

going home

---

journey of dreams

With Thanx

mark j.t. griffin

First Printed in 1999 in Great Britain
Copyright © 1999 by Mark J.T. Griffin

Cover Design

Mark J.T. Griffin
with
Thanks to Alwyn Clayden and Raphael Preston

Published and Distributed by :

Mindwork Ltd
Smithy Croft
Schivas
Ythanbank, Ellon
Aberdeenshire AB41 7UA
Scotland GB

ISBN 0-9533017-0-2 (First Edition)

Printed in Scotland
by
Xpress Print, Graphix House, Wellington Circle, Aberdeen, AB12 3JG

Contents

For Ann, as Always, with Love

In Memory of my Brother David

To Carl Sagan, a visionary

Acknowledgements

A vision is the child of an idea. Ideas are the children of inspiration.

This book could not have been written without the help, encouragement and support of many and there are many without whom ideas could not have been transformed into print.

I would therefore like to acknowledge the following for their motivation, stimulation, guidance, help or contribution to the development of this book :

Ann for her love, patience, encouragement and the spark !

Jack Black and Mindstore, Nancy Paul and David Tyrell, Dave Sherritt
Vangelis, Jon Anderson and Yes
Fish and Marillion, Neil Peart and Rush
Roger Waters, David Gilmour and Pink Floyd
John Wetton and Asia, Genesis, Mike Oldfield
Michael Moorcock, Douglas Adams, Anne McCaffrey
Spike Milligan, Monty Python, Terry Pratchett
Ridley Scott, Luc Besson, Robin Williams, Billy Connolly
Elisabeth Ettrup, Jane Hamby, Heather Wright
Alasdair & Aileen, Alywn & Vesna, Raphael & Paula, Bill & Gaynor
The Griffin and Kinnear Families

Bramble and Bracken who, like all cats,
seem to know something, but aren't saying...

and of course for the energy...

ALL THE VISIONARIES

Author's Note

Some years ago I wrote the first and only biography about the Greek musician Vangelis. The book was a work of fact and having written many short stories it became a dream to write a work of fiction. Now this book is complete I realise it is inevitably a combination of fiction and fact and that *going home* has been an apprenticeship.

A writer is influenced by a combination of personal inputs drawn from history and the media, from childhood and family, from peers and friends and from the facets that makes you the soul and person you are. The characters in *going home* are an amalgam of people from my past with a dash of imagination thrown into the mix. Some of the events in the story occurred and I have altered the perception from which characters and events are viewed. To arrive at those viewpoints has inevitably been a journey of discovery.

As children we are gifted with an imagination to navigate an ocean of dreams and ideas. It is unfortunate that as we voyage through teenage years into adulthood, education and conformity are loaded onto us and our creative spirit is suffocated in favour of the academic, the logical and the rational.

If a book illustrates anything it proves that imagination is fundamental. Without it we may be incomplete and intellectually sterile. With it, mankind has a powerful tool that, used to its full potential, can allow us to journey to the stars, span chasms, climb the highest mountains and perhaps write stories to ignite the imagination of others.

Vision is the key ! Unlock your imagination, visualise your dreams and focus all the power of will and desire to attain them.

going home has been a joy to write. For me it was a vision that I have steered toward as a beacon and I hope that you, the reader, find it as enjoyable and interesting to read, as I found it to research and write.

Once again, many thanks to my friends, family and *beacons in the darkness* for turning my dreams into a reality - it would not have been possible without you.

May You Make Your Dreams Last Longer Than The Night.....

Prologue

Let me share some ideas with you.

There are many who see no value in books and do not take the trouble to read stories such as this one. There are still others who will not discuss the after life, whether through disinterest or fear.

A book, such as the one you hold, is merely a collection of physical signs and symbols pressed onto paper, but it has the power to take you on a personal journey, providing the chance to travel back with and listen to the voice of an author who may have perhaps left this earth centuries before.

It will inevitably be an uncertain journey of the imagination - an individual experience.

A journey that begins, proceeds and ends with ideas.

In contrast, the journey we will all take to the next world is a certain one. Each one of us will make it . It is as sure and certain as the print on the pages of this book.

But, as I write this text I am struck by a disconcerting possibility. These words may be merely the dictation of another author and perhaps I am no more than an earth bound scribe. Perhaps these words are not mine ?

The concept of unearthly manipulation is an ancient one and manipulation by other forces guide our whole lives. Manipulation by the state, by our employers, by our spouses, by our parents, by even ourselves. Should we worry that those of another dimension might wish to do the same ?

Some suggest that our lives are mapped by forces that were ordained long since. The successes and failures of our ancestors, parents and strangers unconsciously guide our decisions and our fate and we are pushed and pulled by the past, by the present and even the *unwritten* future that holds the destiny of our souls.

Many human societies believe in the eternity of the spirit on its infinite journey of learning and climbing the ladder of knowledge. If this is the case, all that we are, all that we discover and all that we do, has purpose and will live on.

Is it not comforting to know that the goals we have not achieved in this life may be attained in a future existence ?

So, why should the spirits of the next world be the least bit interested in our petty lives, our own small steps up this stairway to heaven ?

Perhaps they observe with curiosity our struggles and watch as we add new text to that already written ? In our small and simple ways, we also have a line or two to add to the chapters of the eternal story.

One thing is certain.

One day each of us will return home to the stars.

On that day we will have lived our lives.

On that day will have made our contributions and we will depart.

While we were here we will have made our choices and made our marks.

Some come, live and go without a sigh or a whisper, to leave little or no imprint on the pages of life.

Others, with energy and vision, create waves which crash on the shores of time sending songs to echo and reverberate through the centuries.

Each day we must ask ourselves, have I made, can I make such a resonance ? Have I ignored the opportunities presented to me ? Have I let the grains slip through the hour glass for nought ?

Please. Do not let time steal a few more seconds from you.

Reader, this is a story through time and space, across dimensions and generations. It is a story with a tangled thread that may become difficult to unravel. It is one I nevertheless urge and invite you to follow.

Let us begin our journey...

Chapter 1

Voyages of Discovery

"And how could we mere mortals know the night was nothing more than the cloak of sunlight bringing us a time to reflect on our days' failures and successes. How could we know the darkness it brought was a mantle for the spirit shadows."

Jarrat Toldon, Chronicles of the Future

"...And we were heading straight into the shining sun..."

David Gilmour

Elm's Hospice Wolverhampton

Autumn

e lay, propped up and bolstered on a scatter of pillows, his dark sunken eyes barely open. His breathing was shallow. His body, a wasting shell, was alive but his soul was ready, aching to leave the sinking ship - to swim to the shore, beach upon the warm sands of relief and rest.

No one would have blamed him for giving up, over the past few years he had shouldered so much.

The cancer had taken two years to destroy him. The doctors and the specialists had promised miracles. They had made mistakes through indecision, incompetence, ineffectuality and apathy. In the end they had given up. Lacking vision they had given in to the frustration of a hopeless case. Why give a dying young man a few more months of painful life ? Why put off the inevitable ? The poor *bastard* is dead already - he's terminal.

Finally, in their frustration, they had given him no hope.

So now, to free the bed, they had been gradually murdering him, humanely, of course. An extra milligram of morphine everyday, until his body couldn't feel and his mind didn't care.

They thought that he'd have been dead two weeks before but, he was stronger than that. He was waiting for the right moment, perhaps to be a thorn in their sides for just a while longer to remind them of their ineptitude.

His room was clinical white, clean and off-ward, away from the others. The window had a view of the tops of poplar trees swaying in the September breeze. Under the window was a radiator. It was turned full on making the room unbearably hot. On the bedside table was an assortment of Get-Well cards, a jug of orange squash and a huge bouquet of carnations in an imitation cut glass vase.

On the opposite wall was a pseudo religious picture of a dove rising in flight. Most of the room was a blur to him, but strangely this picture he could see and he focused on it with enormous clarity.

He opened his eyes slightly and could see something white like an angel standing over him. He could feel the warmth of its presence next to him. He could detect a slight perfume. He thought she was holding his hand. He could sense the pinprick in his arm, the warmth of the angel leave his side and felt himself slip another inch into slumber.

Then out of the haze there was a voice he knew.

"Daniel ?" It said questioningly calling him, "Daniel ?" His mind searched for recognition and found a match. It was his brother.

Jon sat by the bed holding Daniel's hand. His brother's fingers were grey, the nails white, his brother felt cadaver cold. The flowing mane of blonde hair which Jon thought made him look like a Viking warrior, was no more, reduced by the radiation and chemotherapy to a few thin silk strands combed behind his ears .

Jon looked at his brother's ashen face. Death was written into the lines and Jon realised his brother had no more than a few days and would be gone .

Jon's love for his brother was not particularly special or deep, it was no more or less than any brother's, but to see a fellow human struggle for each breath wrenched at his heart. Jon squeezed Daniel's hand, more out of comfort for himself than for his brother. Daniel turned his head slightly, his eyes still shut and with an effort he spoke.

"Don't be afraid Jon" he whispered, "I'm ready. I've been ready since they told me two years ago, only cowardice made me stay."

"You were never so...", Jon said losing the words and gripping Daniel's hand tighter, "I could never have taken what you've endured."

Daniel smiled wearily, "You have no choice. You become dependant, addicted and unable to escape. Its the drugs that make you brave, if they didn't you'd lose your mind."

There was a pregnant silence until Daniel broke it. "So how I am looking ?" He asked with a smile.

Jon relaxed realising Daniel's humour, "Well, I've seen you look better." He said in reply.

They both smiled at each other in agreement. Jon then remembered an earlier visit and searched just under the bed. He found what he was looking for and lifted the ring pull on the can of beer strategically placed on the floor beneath the bed by one of the hospital porters. He poured a little of it onto Daniel's drying lips.

"I could really put this stuff away once !" Daniel said tasting the few drops on his dry tongue that he had managed to imbibe.

Looking at his brother enjoying a simple can of beer made Jon silent and agitated. He felt he should be strong and stoic for the patient. If the truth were known Jon didn't have the courage or the bravery. There were so many things he wanted to say but, Daniel said them for him.

"Jon. Don't worry. I know what you want to tell me. You feel the sorrow, the pain that I once felt." Daniel gripped Jon's hand.

Jon stared at his brother's frail body, the result of the medical profession's accepted solution for the situation, the slow and painless poisoning by morphine. Everyone knew, nobody said. And what could Jon say ? Society had found a panacea for its terminally ill. An easy way out - legalised euthanasia.

Daniel released his hand from Jon's grip and stroked Jon's hand. Daniel's face grimaced from this effort.

"I'm looking forward to it you know. Meeting some new faces, getting to see the *Big G* , have a chat with Elvis," Daniel smiled again, "...ask old Mozart if it was Salieri that bumped him off or whether it was just the flu."

Daniel thought a moment and added, "I'm looking forward to it. Up there is no injustice. No pain. No politics. No inhumanity. Pure love. Existence and eternity has meaning !" Daniel gripped Jon's hand to emphasise the point.

Jon had never heard Daniel speak of spiritual things and realised Daniel spoke with sincerity. "Jon. We make mistakes and don't ever learn our lessons."

Jon shook his head and looked into Daniel's watery blue eyes that suddenly became brighter with excitement and anticipation.

"I've seen it Jon. I've seen it ! Its so bloody simple Jon."

Daniel rested back into the pillows and released Jon's hand, raising a finger pointing to a faded tapestry sampler that hung on the opposite wall. Picked out in cross stitch and initialed by the embroiderer it said :

"For evil to triumph it is only enough for good men to do nothing "

A.M.G. 1986

Jon had seen the motto before but had never really thought about it. He stared at it as it etched onto his memory. At that moment the nurse knocked on the door and entered the room. Daniel had slumped back again into silence. The nurse apologised and told Jon it was time to leave.

"Its okay !" Jon said lying badly and trying not to embarrass anyone, "I have to be fly back to Scotland shortly anyway...." He looked down at Daniel. It was almost as if he wasn't there.

"Well Daniel," he said "this is it. I have to make tracks." Jon tried to sound brave but he sounded almost patronising. Jon took Daniel's hand in a hand shake then reached over and stroked his brother's head.

"You take of yourself. I'll see you," he said. Jon could feel grief overwhelming him and he fought it . He suddenly realised in that moment that he may never see his brother again and he stared at him hoping the moment may last longer. Daniel lifted a finger from his limp hand.

He voice was now just a whisper, "See you soon Jon. Remember brother, be a good man..." Jon turned to go and Daniel spoke as he turned for a last glance at his brother, "Until the next time Jon ? Until the next time ?"

Jon smiled, "...until the next time..." he agreed.

Two days later, on a warm, bright and golden September's afternoon Daniel died peacefully at the hospice with his mother at his bedside.

And as the light began to fade then grow brighter, his thoughts were that somewhere in the corner of the universe a star in some distant and dying constellation exploded into supernova and in that brief moment was the brightest light in all the cosmos.

Queenstown Ireland

11th April 1912

The boat had taken twenty minutes to cross the narrow stretch of water out to the vessel where it was moored two miles from the pier. As the launch approached the ship the wall of the hull loomed above them and they were struck with awe at her vastness.

The journey had been tinged with sadness and people seemed to be lost in their thoughts as they tied up at the side of the liner.

As they disembarked, Eric Matheson and his family were the last of the 113 3rd Class passengers to step from the tenders.

Eric had long dreamed of going to America. To seek his fortune. To build a better life for himself and his family. He held his wife Katherine and twin daughters close and they gazed out across the ocean and watched the coast of Ireland drift into the haze.

He dipped into his waistcoat pocket and pulled out the watch his father had given him as a leaving present. He thought of the parents he left behind and the sadness in his mother's eyes. He thought of his friends and the farewell party they had thrown for them. He thought of his future and his dream of prosperity in a new land.

He had studied hard in Dublin and his doctor's practice in Knocklinn had flourished or at least enough for him to be able to save a little. He knew a better future was before him. The colonialism of Britain cast a shadow on his beloved Ireland that perhaps one day would be lifted.

As a young doctor he hoped he could set up a new practice in Chicago where his younger brother had settled some years before. He was torn between losing his family and his country and the search for a secure future. America would perhaps give him this.

The journey ahead of them would not be long, just a couple of weeks, but it was one he did not relish cramped in the 3rd Class cabins below the waterline. In the luxury of the decks above him the 1st Class passengers travelled in oak lined opulence with chandeliers, waiters and smoked salmon. His beloved Katherine deserved as much. One day they would travel in the same style.

"Well ladies" he said smiling at his family warmly, "shall we go below to the warmth of the engines and our private suites ? There's quite a chill in the air."

The two girls scurried on ahead excited of their new surroundings. Eric squeezed his wife's hand and kissed her tenderly on the cheek.

"Eric !" she said wriggling in embarrassment, "you should not be so bold ! People will talk !"

He laughed, "About a husband kissing his pretty wife ! Ach, away with you my sweet Kathy !" And he threw an arm around her waist, "come on, let's find something to eat."

As he descended the steps below he took out a cigarette from the silver case his wife had given him on their wedding day and lit it. Closing it, he fingered his initials, E.M. , that she had had engraved on the lid and his heart glowed with the thought of their wedding day. The dancing, the music, the laughter, the singing, the jigs all whirled in his head.

From the decks below he could hear musicians playing an old tune on a fiddle and dulcimer that he had known from childhood - "Paddy Ryan's Dream". A lilting piece evoking memories. The waltzing tune seemed to capture the moment, a great love tinged with the sadness and apprehension of the future.

It danced in his head, exciting his thoughts and returning him to the smoky hall where he'd first danced with sweet Katherine. He wanted to be close to the sound and he squeezed his wife's waist ,stepping briskly down the nearest staircase.

They could hear the music on the deck below but took a few moments to find the source. They were still finding their way around what was a maze of stairways and corridors all of which seemed to look the same, but, it was certainly an impressive vessel all the same. Eric remembered the wide eyed thrill of his nephew Sean when he heard his uncle, aunt and cousins would be travelling on the mighty "Titanic".

Bristol, England

1481

It was a cold and wintry summer's day as two Genoese navigators stood on the docks at Bristol slightly tired after their journey across England from Dover. The next stage of their journey would be far more treacherous.

They had scoured the docks for most of the morning searching for suitable passage, a trader heading to the Norwegian colonies of Vinland in search of pelts, salt-fish and walrus tusks.

The captain had been agreeable but a price could only he negotiated with the owner. The captain introduced them.

"Senor Colon, I would like to introduce the owner of this vessel - Mr John Jay."

Hands were extended and greetings exchanged.

"So, sir, you and your brother require passage on 'The Spirit'. Can I ask your purpose ? It is not often we have a request for passage on a vessel such as ours - salt-fish is not the sweetest of travelling companions !"

Christoph Colon smiled. He found the English humour difficult to understand and he was still getting used to the intricacies of its language.

"I am sure I can trust your discretion sir. Bartholemo and myself are conducting a geographic and navigational survey. It is our belief that a short passage exists between the West and the Indies which could save many months sailing."

Jay found Colon very direct but honest. Some owners would have thought the men lunatics or heretics. Jay felt he too should be direct.

"And how does sailing to the Vinland colonies help you with that ?"

Colon was guarded but told him enough to interest the man.

"It is quite simple. For many years we have known the existence of a map which showed land or islands to the south of these colonies. Some of our research leads us to believe that these islands are on route to the Indies or are the east edge of the Indies. The original map makers were Norwegian Vikings and we believe they may have information which may expand our knowledge.."

"It is an interesting premise. We have an Icelander who is our navigator. I am sure he can be of some assistance. Indeed, I myself would of course be interested in such a mission. Come let us discuss the project further out of this wind," and he led them below.

Jay was still a little suspicious of two foreigners hiring his vessel. Their English, other than the Italian accent was perfect and he decided he should delve deeper, "Incidentally sirs, your English is good. Have you been in Bristol some time ?"

Christoph smiled, "No Mr Jay. We have quite a mixed upbringing. Gaelic of the Scots is actually our mother tongue - our parents were originally from the West Highlands. We were born on the small Isle of Iona in the land of St Columba. Our father was a navigator and sailor by trade. The family moved at first to southern Ireland then on to Brittany and from there eventually to Genoa where we adopted the name Colon. Our family name is actually derived from St Columba. It is Columbus."

Chapter 2

Views of the Gateway

"And when they found that the spirits, the souls of the unrested, were influencing and shaping lives, men were not surprised, but angry. For they came to us when we were at rest, as they should have been. They invaded our safest of places. They violated our dreams."

Jarrat Toldon, Chronicles of the Future

*"Truth is after all a moving target, hairs to split and pieces that don't fit
How can anyone be enlightened ? Truth is after all so poorly lit"*

Neil Peart

Aberdeenshire

Autumn - 1998

he Smithy had stood for over 250 years, battered and torn by the bitter east wind and the drenching ice cold rain. Each stone could tell a story, each brick held a memory, each slate echoed a raindrop.

Father to son, the Smithy had been passed through the generations earning a sufficient living for the men that had worked in it but, then came the progress of the 1900's. By the time the car had replaced the horse the Smithy had become the monument it was now, a colourful granite shell lit up against the bleak skyline. Early in the century it had been a barn, a home for the mice and finally, ironically a garage but, the Smithy still remembered the old days. MacGregor, the last of his line and long dead, remembered the old days .

Jon and his wife Ann had moved into the nearby Croft two years previously. Though they owned the building the Smithy would never really be theirs, they were simply the current custodians. The acre of land they occupied for their lifetimes - for no man can own land - took in the Smithy and they used it as a loft overflow, shed and garage when the weather turned winter white.

For much of the time, the Smithy was just "there", taken for granted, part of the scenery. The possibilities of conversion into a cottage were explored, but discounted through lack of money. Jon diligently mowed around it and kept the building free of rodents, maybe slowing the decay and stopping it falling down.

Until one Sunday.

Jon had completed his usual gardening chores round the grounds. He had cut the grass using his trusty but rusty 'sit and ride' mower and was throwing the dust cover over the machine when something, maybe the sound of the dust blowing through the doors, or the creak of a roof beam as it sighed with age, made him stop. For perhaps the first time he looked at the old building in a new light.

He gazed up at the joists and the many housemartin's nests between them. He stared at the myriad colours, greys, yellows, pinks and silvers in the old worn and shabby granite stones, solid and silent. He rubbed his hands over the sooty hearth where once stood the blacksmith and the scorching fires of the furnace. Above him the rusty wheels and leather bands of the bellows and turning gear were thick with cobwebs. In the corner the old well, its contents brackish and green and its top covered by a grate to stop the neighbourhood cats losing a life.

He wandered over to the ladder and climbed up to the loft space to the what was once the bothy. He imagined the apprentice and blacksmith sitting on the floor in front of the fire drinking beer, laughing and playing cards. The floor boards were covered thick dust and stacked in the corner were a pile of old newspapers.

They were all from the early sixties. He picked the first and read the headline.

KENNEDY WINS NOMINATION

Jon cast it back on the pile and thought that a good Sunday afternoon bonfire was certainly overdue. Another job for another day.

Through dirty dormer windows he could see across the rape fields now ready for harvest and above them the dark storm clouds gathering for another Grampian downpour. On the other side of the bothy and through another dormer he could make out the hill of Bennachie some 20 miles way that was already shrouded in the mist of teeming rain .

Jon carefully climbed back down the ladder and clapped the dust off his hands then wiped them on an old piece of rag that had been tied to the 12th rung of the ladder.

He took a last look around and decided to go and brew up. He walked through the old doors back across the courtyard to the Croft.

Then they came to him, "come and visit again....yes...remember us again......" the voices whispered.

Jon stopped and turned, thinking he had heard someone he looked around the building again. His spine tingled in anticipation but he could only hear the sound of silence and smell of the damp dust. He resolved it must have been the wind and an over active imagination. With an effort he shut and bolted the oak doors and crossed back to the Croft for a hot drink.

That night, though tired, Jon slept restlessly. Something gnawed at his conscience. The wind and rain battered on the roof and rattled the roof tiles. He finally got to sleep and began to lapse into dreams. And he dreamt.

He saw himself above his sleeping form, floating, drifting, flying. The bedroom seemed to have no ceiling and he drifted higher and higher until the earth seemed far below him. It seemed to him that he was flying free, high above the sleeping world. And in flight he heard a voice.

"Jon....", It said, "..it is me. Daniel..." It was his brother.

"Daniel ?" Jon said searching for a path through his confusion, "where am I ? I am...? But, you're...."

"Dead ? No ! I'm, shall we say *elsewhere*...we have to talk."

There seemed to be irony and greeting in the voice. He had expected the latter but not the former from a ghost.

"Do you really exist ?" Jon asked tentatively.

"I'm as real as you are !" Daniel said defensively, "you exist, don't you ?"

"I guess I do," Jon replied, "...I know its a little Cartesian but I think therefore I am !"

"Good ! I'm glad we agree," Somehow, Jon sensed his brother sit and relax, "now to business ! Jon I've been told to explain something to you, its just that I don't think you realise what you have close to your home. It's one of the most powerful gateways in the multi-verse. You must...be...wary...of....."

His brother's voice started to fade and Jon felt himself drifting again and then falling like a rock. He was accelerating though the air and felt himself drawn back to earth by a gravity which for a time appeared to have been absent. He felt himself hit the ground and he returned with a jolt to his sleeping form on the bed. He awoke with a start, sweating in the pitch darkness.

The next morning he felt exhausted but was compelled to be up at first light. With some effort he dragged himself out of bed, his body was tired but his spirit was restless. He dressed and pulled on a coat to walk across the courtyard to the Smithy; subconsciously called there.

A bitter breeze blew back the leaves of dried grass and dust as Jon unbolted and opened the ancient oak Smithy door. As it opened a blast of ice cold air chilled his face.

The dust vortexed up blinding him for an instant and he thought he caught a glimpse of an old man standing before him, white haired and bearded wearing a leather apron. The man carried what appeared to be a pair of forge tongs.

Jon stepped back in surprise and closed his eyes, wiping away the dust. He opened them again and a strange eeriness was all around him. He closed his eyes again through fear and then with apprehension opened them again.

His surroundings were all they had been. Sane, reassuring and normal.

He stepped through the doorway towards the well. Jon stared down into the brackish water and its murky depths. Water dripped from the moss clinging to the walls and caused ripples on the surface of the ice cold water. He switched on his torch and shone it on the water not expecting to see anything. In the watery, black mirror a white ghostly face stared back at him and smiled.

He leapt back with a gasp, trying to catch his breath and dropped the torch leaving him in darkness. Fumbling about on the ground he eventually found it and turned it back on. He stepped gingerly forward to the edge of the well and slowly followed the torch beam down the side as the damp granite and green moss reflected florescent in the light; the beam coming to rest once more on the surface of the water.

There was nothing but the ripples lapping against the mossy granite sides mirror pitch blackness, cold and silent as a grave.

London

May 1972

On the top floor of one of the highest of the penthouse towers that lined the Thames South of Tower Bridge two maintenance men stepped from the lift on the 30th floor and went about their business. They walked cautiously down the empty corridor carrying tool boxes and a large aluminium case. It was nine in the morning and most of the occupants were at work, they were looking for Apartment 3005. They stopped outside the door and knocked, waiting for a reply but expecting none. They knocked again with the same response. Across the corridor in Flat 3007 Radio One blared out its banal morning show.

"Bloody Dave Lee Travis," one of them whispered.

One of the two quickly opened the toolbox and removed a small brown bottle. Unscrewing the lid with its pipette, he carefully sucked up some of the liquid in the bottle and squeezed it into the lock of door 3005. The lock fizzed as the chemical reaction worked on the mechanism. He tried the door handle and it opened.

They stepped into the flat. Its windows had a spectacular view over the river and the city of London. They entered the spacious sitting room and made for the large painting they knew would be hanging over the fireplace. Without ceremony they removed it from the wall. The wall behind it appeared blank and faded but closer examination revealed a seam running down the centre. Probing the seam with a pen knife they located the latch and it sprung open to reveal a safe. A few tense minutes later they had the safe door open and were eagerly scanning the interior.

On the bottom shelf were a few envelopes of cash, a little jewellery and some papers. The top shelf held a number of small boxes, parcels and packages wrapped in paper or plastic, one of which fitted diagonally across the inside of the safe. Their instructions were to remove any packages without concern for their contents so they hurriedly transferred the objects into their aluminium suit case. After closing first the safe, then the wall cupboard door and rehanging the picture on its hook, they crossed to the apartment door pausing a moment to listen for movement. They stepped into the corridor, closing the apartment door quietly behind them and walked purposefully to the stairwell leading to a rear exit from the building, their mission successfully completed. Twenty minute's work had earned them half a million, much more than their previous military salaries.

Within the hour the aluminium case and its contents were concealed in a crate at Heathrow and it was on its way to the old man in Vienna.

Mons Grampius Caledonia

Harvest Time 51AD

They had come as devils in the night and they had not know what hit them until it was too late. The hill fort of Ben Achie had been utterly destroyed and the homes of their fortified huts were now blazing, their women and children dead or dying. The Picts had retreated to the protection of the higher ground that looked over the Grampian mountains to the West and the sea on the horizon to the East. They were now fighting for survival on the marshy open ground .

Macordon could not understand the fates. The fort had been well defended and he had thought that today the gods were with them. He had been wrong. The invaders had attacked without warning - he knew his wife, children mother, father were already dead. He had seen his brother butchered like a beast by two of the warriors. He realised the dead were the lucky ones.

The battle raged but, Caesar's war hardened, disciplined men were invincible - against the unorganised Caledonian Picts of Macordon. The Picts would rally and attack, but the Romans would fight back with twice the ferocity. It was as if the enemy fed from the aggression and it made them ever stronger. Wave after wave of warriors bore down on the ranks of courageous, brave but doomed Picts.

The Roman commander Orelius had been on the Britannic campaign for three years. He knew his men and how far they could be pushed. He had got to know the country and the guerrilla tactics of the enemy. Above all he knew the brutal wrath of his command for failure. He never feared defeat but, today he knew the gods were with them.

He gave the order to break ranks sensing easy slaughter, victory and the enemy routed. With a command from Orelius they were upon the now retreating enemy, cutting, hacking, slashing all in their path - no quarter, no mercy, no prisoners, no survivors - only the quick would not perish.

The Picts scattered in all directions desperate to escape, screaming for mercy. They dashed down the hill of Ben Achie hoping to make the cover of the vast forest that covered the ridge of the hill.

Macordon, sensing the end was close, cried to his men to run for the cover and the partial defence of a rocky outcrop. He ran for his life, stumbling over the uneven ground.

Turning to check that his son was still behind him he saw him cut down from behind by a Roman blade. He screamed in rage but it drew the attention of Orelius who, scenting blood, rode after the escaping Scot.

Between Macordon and the rocks was the village border stone carved with runes that marked the edge of the clan's territory and at which the camp sacrificed to the gods at harvest time. If he could make it to the stone he was sure the gods would give him strength and protect him.

Macordon ran, tears in his eyes but before he had run twenty yards he stumbled and rolled into the soaking wet bracken. He desperately tried to find his feet and felt himself pushed back to the ground by a booted foot. He rolled over and gazed up in terror at the dark face before him.

"So. Where are your idols today Pict ?" The voice raged, thrusting down with the standard and running Macordon through, his back now against the cold Pict stone.

Macordon felt the searing pain in his stomach and felt the numbing cold of death envelop him. He felt tears in his eyes and the blood seeping from his veins and with cold now running through his body he cursed the murderer of his family and died.

And in death he heard the gods singing to him.

* * * * *

Every night we dream. Collating and filing thoughts and aspirations, righting the wrongs of the day, re-battling lost moments and easing guilty consciences. Sometimes our dreams are so vivid that we feel they are not dreams at all but films in which we have the leading role. In sleep it seems we are sometimes perilously close to disaster, the edge of a precipice, in front of a firing squad, about to die, until we are woken, gasping for breath, sweating and trying to make sense in the darkness of our twisted mind's invention.

On our planet, spinning like a jewel in the darkness, two people dream connected by a thread. In San Francisco a young man naps in the cool breeze on the grass of Golden Gate park. In Stuttgart a woman slumbers in the warmth of an apartment within the sound of the late night S-bahn.

Then like a clap of thunder and a blinding white flash of light, they awake as if on cue, shaken out of sleep by something in their dreams the power of which is beyond their comprehension and which will move and change their mundane and purposeless lives.

In London the incessant hum of traffic disturbs another restless night of a third who rarely sleeps. An adversary has also awakened to his purpose.

* * * * *

23

Jon sat at the kitchen table watching the rain and nursing a mug of hot coffee spiked with Glenfiddich. He felt its warmth course through his veins and glow in his stomach. He was trying to make some sense of the last few hours, his dream and the visions in the Smithy. He could not remember the whole conversation with his brother but, he remembered feelings, thoughts, warmth and love.

As he watched the rain trickle down the windows he wondered if he could be going insane. Alone, he was beginning to hear voices in his sleep and see things that made no sense. His mind drowsy with the alcohol combined with the hypnotic pattering of the rain, he drifted into a light slumber and once again began to dream.

"Jon ? How do you feel..?" A voice asked calmly.

Jon spoke through a haze, "lousy..." He said "...but then again its not often you get to speak to your dead brother. Maybe you're not..."

"Jon, I am. You know it." The humour in his brother's voice was gone, "Jon. You're going to think this irrational but heaven is missing some angels !"

"I'm sorry ?" Jon was dumbfounded.

"I don't know how else to put it" Daniel paused for thought, "The eternal book is out of balance. There are a number of us who we can not account for."

"But ? How can that be ?" Jon was flabbergasted.

"We think they've been 'misdirected' we're not sure. We've got some of the best minds working on it but we need your help."

"Okay. So why me ? Surely you've got Einstein, Newton and quite a few others to help," Jon retorted flippantly.

"Yeah ! Very funny," Daniel answered sarcastically, "we know you've a good mind for this sort of stuff. You're a problem solver, computer programmer. You were always tenacious, Jon." Daniel thought for a moment and said, "just follow up some of the ideas we've got here and see how you go."

Jon thought for a moment and then asked, "This is a dream isn't....??"

"It's..what...ever...you....wish it...to be...." and the voice faded again.

He awoke with a jolt as his coffee mug smashed on the stone floor.

Chapter 3

Reminders of the Past

"When the voices would not stop we prayed for their ending and we pleaded for peace, but the spirit shadows could not be silenced. They were of another world and they had purpose."

Jarrat Toldon, Chronicles of the Future

"Once we did love ! How we chased a millions stars and touched as only one."

Jon Anderson

Stuttgart, Germany

Schlossplatz is a grand square bordered by a magnificent baroque palace and an old medieval baronial hall. At its centre is a column to liberty and the glory of the German people surrounded by a colourful garden of roses, marigolds and geraniums. Koenigstrasse cuts the top of the square with a covered facade under which the street cafes spill their clientele out onto the steps to sit under white umbrellas, at crisp blue table cloths.

At the one end of the square the archway of the nave portal, standing stark against the skyline, is the only remains of the old dorf church of Stuttgart destroyed during an apocalyptic rain of bombs during the winter of 1943.

Annelise sat at the end table, people watching. She observed as a voyeuse fascinated by the characters; the beggar after a few pfennig, the busker singing his appalling Bob Dylan medley and the shoppers like blinkered automatons chasing one material desire or another.

She sipped at her second coffee, flicking through Die Welt. The sun shone scorchingly on the August day baking the *"beamters"* as they took an hour away from the intense enjoyment of paper shuffling and bureaucracy.

The sun tanned her olive skin that suited her blonde hair and electric blue eyes. She enjoyed the sunshine and she knew that men noticed her at this table, indeed she had selected the table in order that they may.

As she emptied her mind of the morning's problems, wrestling with the cities planning and architecture at the Staatsamt, the bright blue skies suddenly darkened as if a storm was about to break. She folded her newspaper prepared to run for shelter and was puzzled that no one else seemed to have noticed it.

And the scene changed, melting like candle wax into a grotesque and vivid sepia tableau.

People ran screaming, an old lady dashed toward on old building off the square, the church - an old chapel. Bodies lay across rubble, fire blazed and the bombs fell with a banshee scream. British planes strafed the skies unchallenged, meeting no resistance from the Luftwaffe. Death, damnation and destruction rained down.

Annelise sat frozen in her seat, protected by a bubble that enveloped her as she watched the carnage, completely powerless to react.

Suddenly an incredible flash engulfed the square and wiped out any life in it. It destroyed the chapel and all inside it leaving just the arch of the door standing starkly against the quiet skies.

And the scene changed again...

Shoppers with carrier bags, children with ice creams, dogs and their owners and the busker - a typical August day. Annelise shook herself from the waking dream. Had anyone else experienced it ? Had anyone else viewed the same metamorphosis ? Something had briefly opened a window on the past.

* * * * *

Jon seated himself in his favourite carver chair gathering warmth and comfort in front of the crackling glow of the open fire. The last few days had affected him severely and he felt as if he was going insane. He struggled to rationalise the voices. He felt alone but the fire and alcohol warmed him. He thought back to his youth, a bright and reassuring time, when he and his brother had the same interests and dreams, hopes and fears.

He gazed into the flames and talked;

"Dave and I were in the same hockey team. One match I will never forget against a team of brawn and no brain. It was a miserable day, the rain was teaming down and the opposition were one-nil ahead with about ten minutes to play. The game was slipping away from us. We knew we could beat them, if we could just get one back maybe we could hold them.

Suddenly, I found myself the glory boy, I was making a run, effortlessly passing everything in my path, only the goalie to beat. Just as I was about to set up the shot I felt a jolt, a push in my back and I fell to the ground, bought down from behind, a skilful foul.

In slo-mo I saw a shadow come round me choosing a spot to clear the ball. I looked up and he grinned at me. A self satisfied smile that gloated at easy victory. I lay there in the mud as he circled me choosing his moment. As I lay there, beaten, trying to find the energy to lift myself up, I heard a shout. It was Daniel calling me, shouting at me."

Jon took another sip of the aqua-vitae.

" 'Jon !' He screamed, 'Jon ! Get up...!' I was out. It was all I could do to notice him, let alone get up ! Again. 'Jon ! Get up ! Get up....Get him....!' I looked up and saw the player silhouetted against the sun. It was the spark that lit the fuse. I felt utter hatred for that shape. I pushed myself up and from somewhere my legs found new energy. 'Yes...' I screamed in anger and was upon him."

Jon smiled as he remembered the day, "Needless to say we won two-one ! The power of the positive !" And Jon looked up at an old and battered white hockey ball mounted on a teak plinth on the mantel piece, a souvenir of the match. He reached up and lifted it off its polished teak plinth. He held the ball in his hands feeling it's indents and scuffs. It bought back memories of his forgotten childhood and of his family but most of all his brother .

"This is difficult" Jon said slumping into the carver , "but I need to tell you...." Jon felt his wife close to him.

"The last thing I remember about my brother," Jon said looking into the fire , "was his smile." Jon could feel a tear welling up into the corner of his eye.

"I knew I wouldn't see him for a long time, I knew he didn't have long" Jon looked with pain into the glowing embers of the hearth, "I wanted to hold him, hug him, comfort him. I can't even remember if I did. All I can remember was his thin blond hair and stroking my hands thorough it."

Jon felt his wife hold him. He cried, it was the first time since their parting that he could get out the pain and grief of loss but he knew Daniel, who had been so full of life, would not want sadness or grief.

In his heart Jon could hear his wife playing the piano. Consumed with tiredness and with Beethoven's Moonlight Sonata easing his sadness Jon slept.

* * * * *

Stunned and in a trance Annelise had made it onto the S-bahn for home. She didn't seem to notice the grey faces of the people engrossed in their newspapers, cigarettes and themselves.

This was what she abhorred about commuting. An hour of being rocked gently by the diddle-dee-dee-diddle-dee-dum in cramped stuffy carriages, often standing. Packing people into the carriage like cattle trucks was inhumane, sobering to think that if cattle were treated the same there would be an outcry !

Her mind wandered on the wasted time of it all. She pondered on the mental arithmetic that told her she spent two days every month just travelling to and from work. Surely there was a higher purpose ? Once again her mind returned to the vision she had had earlier, trying to rationalise and dissect it.

Preoccupied as she was, it wasn't until she was close to home she realised she had got off the S-bahn and begun to climb the hill to her apartment block. She walked backwards up the hill swinging her bag in front of her and gazed over the lights of the city trying to mark out the landmarks of the Alte Schloss, Koenigstrasse and the Bahnhof tower with its neon Mercedes sign turning lazily.

In the distance, she heard the hum of the city hum, it's traffic feeding the autobahns as a life's blood. She felt the claustrophobic weight of thousands of lives too close to the next, yearning for individuality.

Annelise reached the comfort of her flat and opened the windows and shutters to let the stagnant air out and the cool night air in. She needed to relax and to think.

She still felt rather shaky and exhausted from her vision. Turning the vivid manifestation over in her mind, she felt as if the scene were familiar to her but she could not understand why this should be. She sat on the bed and leaned back closing her eyes to think.

And in the twilight state between day dream and deep slumber she slept.

She felt herself slipping away and drifting, floating upwards. She felt tired, weary and heavy yet her soul floated like a cloud. As she sailed on an ocean of air a voice came to her.

"Annelise. Remember me, " the voice in her dream said "remember that day we were parted." Annelise stirred but still slept. "We were walking in the square, talking about what we would do when the fighting stopped. Remember ? It ended for us both that day. I stayed and you returned again. It's me Annelise. It's Reinhardt. Remember."

She plumbed the depths of her memories and realised somehow what the voice said was true. She searched her heart and could feel love, warmth and passion.

"I had so much more to learn, my love. But, you returned. I stayed."

She searched for reason and tried desperately to speak, "I don't understand."

"You progressed. You learned hope. But, now it is time for reason and logic. The heart and the mind as one. You are lucky. It is now your seventh time on this earth."

Annelise, with a flash of realisation understood what the voice was saying. Images of many times and many lives flickered in her mind like a movie, the plot, characters and script of which were instantly recognisable.

"Annelise, do you remember our favourite piece ? The piece we heard in the cathedral on the night we parted ?"

Out of the mist Annelise could see a baroque Dom, golden, lavish paintings, the smell of incense, the memories so long ago but so clear. She heard grand music, music to stir the soul and let the spirit soar. It was Mozart.

"Yes, my love ! Mozart ! The Requiem !" the voice said.

* * * * *

Jon was now very drunk. He had never taken alcohol very well. The bottle of Glenfiddich was now almost empty. He felt bitter, angry, full of self pity but most of all, very drunk.

"Bastards," he said to anyone who might be listening, "bastards making me crazy. Sending bloody ghosts to make me crazy. Bastards !" He tried to raise himself up but his hand slipped from the arm of the chair and he slid back into the seat again.

"I've had enough ! Talking to me in my sleep. Crazy bastards, what right have they got. It's got to stop." He began a drunken rant. "It's got to bloody stop. They can leave me alone" and, enraged, he threw the bottle at the fire. It smashed against the mantel piece splashing glass and whiskey on the hearth and making the fire flare dangerously into life.

Suddenly the old hockey ball flew off its plinth and hit the opposite wall with incredible impact. It bounced off the wall and rebounded on the floor, knocking over a can of coke spilling the liquid left in the can. The ball rolled to his feet with a final spin of defiance.

He looked down at it, took hold of it and held it up to the light. Jon suddenly felt very, very sober, "shit," he whispered under his breath.

That night Jon's head hit the pillow and he slept soundly. He felt in control and this time he was ready for his brother. In sleep he entered the dream state and floated toward self consciousness.

"You got my message then ?" the voice asked, "dramatic wasn't it ?"

"You bet ! Scared the shit out of me." Jon said.

"Sorry, but you needed a shock. You never were very responsive under the influence."

"What do you want me to do ?"

"We'll let you know. We'll guide you where we can and act on what you find. We have someone else who will help you too in case things get dangerous."

"What shall I do first ?"

"Can't you guess ? I gave you a clue !" Again there was humour, a teasing quality in the voice. It was obvious that Jon had no idea what Daniel was intimating. Daniel gave him a stronger hint, "The coke can. Now, what city do you know with a landmark coke can ?" Daniel said and his voice faded into the darkness.

"Birmingham !" Jon said to himself.

Chapter 4

Going on is Going Far

"It is said that men return to this plane over and over again, to learn and learn again, climbing a spiritual ladder. On every visit we learn a new lesson or perhaps fail a test. For the successful another aspect of life is learnt. For the failures....."

Jarrat Toldon, Chronicle of the Future

"This problem seems insoluble. The answer is impossible. All logic ceases to exist. Emotion is the thing we miss !"

Asia

San Francisco

t was a hot day for San Francisco a city used to the constant chill rolling off the Pacific. People with time to spare filled the sidewalk cafes and Fisherman's Wharf to drink cold beer and eat ice cream.

Drew walked amongst the tourists and walked down to watch the seals that basked on the marina next to the wharf. The pungent perfume of hundreds of seals being fed by the tourists on a hot sticky day lead Drew to find a quiet cafe when he could read his newspaper and view the Bay, the Golden Gate and Alcatraz. He fed the juke box and ordered a coke light.

Drew enjoyed finishing work early on a Friday to come down to the wharf and gaze across the bay. At his last birthday, the big "three oh", he felt a change of life style was in order and so rather than dashing home to dash out again he spent some quality time down at the quay and unwound for the weekend. He sighed and ran his fingers through his thin blonde hair, removing his glasses to remove a smudge from them.

And like the melting of a polythene bag in a furnace the scene changed...

Suddenly the dock shook, the waves in the bay began to swell and the earth shook. On the quayside people began to panic and run for shelter. Drew was frozen in his seat unable to escape the tumult. In the distance he could hear screams, the occasional explosion, cries, car brakes screeching, sirens and then the ground shook more violently. He looked out across the bay. The Golden Gate shuddered and the sea raged.

The bridge span swayed drunkenly and Drew gasped a one of the central sections dropped, depositing cars like toys into the foaming sea. Along the arc of the bay bathers sheltered dumb struck on the beach.

Turning around to the city he could see the buildings shake, the tip of the Trans Am building broke and began to fall. The windows in the buildings close to him shattered and there were more explosions. A section of the freeway feeding the heart of the city collapsed like a row of dominoes derailing a tram that careered through the barrier into a building on Ness.

And then the rumble became a murmur and then an eerie silence.

And the scene changed...

The music on the juke box grew louder, the tourists took photos and fed the seals.

Back in his apartment Drew sat on the balcony over looking Coit Tower trying to make sense of his vision. He could not figure it out. He had gone over the vision from the afternoon again and again. He watched it in his mind's eye freezing each frame as video, the picture clear and vivid.

He thought it looked like a San Francisco of perhaps ten years in the future. The boats and cars seemed a little more futuristic and part of the skyline was unknown to him. He knew it was some premonition of catastrophe but who could he report it to ? People would say he was crazy. After all, that was what he was beginning to think himself.

Some hours later Drew lazed in his wicker chair and listened to some jazz rock. He had been drinking a bottle of German wine and it had gone to his head. He felt drugged, drowsy, drunk and dopey. He sat back in his chair and closed his eyes and slept.

"Drew. Do not be afraid." The voice in his dream spoke. Brilliant white light blinded him and from it a voice of infinity spoke to him.

"Drew. It was me, I sent you the message. It was a gift."

"But why ? What gift ?" He knew that he dreamt but had no will to wake himself.

"The images of San Francisco. Friday August 23rd 2012."

"But, for what reason ? Why do you...."

"Simple Drew. So you and yours can be safe at that time. A warning that you must be safe !"

There was a whispering silence and then the voice spoke again, "I want you to take a journey," the voice said. "I need you and your talents to help two others with the same."

"Talents ?"

"....questions, questions, always questions. It is good. Drew you are a visionary. I have visited your dream to help bridge your world with mine, what you would call between the after life. We call it the *Wait State*. Drew, I want you to travel first to the wilderness of Yosemite. There is something there you must see, to reinforce these ideas you will want proof. Begin your journey soon," and the voice began to fade.

"Wait ! Wait ! What is your name ? What do they call you ?"

"I have had many names Drew. I have been Jarrold Karrafet. Jahpur Khan but you probably know me as John Fitzgerald Kennedy..."

* * * * *

Jon had finally realised the significance of his experiences of the last few days. He was being guided, moved towards goals of which he had no idea. He needed to think, to walk, to be alone and he drove to the small cove of Collieston Bay. Last century it had bustled with small fishing vessels but now it was a sleepy dormitory village for the oil and granite grey city of Aberdeen.

Jon parked and walked down onto the beach to be with the sea and the crashing waves of the ocean. He kicked a stone and watched it roll and draw random patterns in the sand. He saw how his footprints filled with foaming water behind him and he felt a calming peace come over him.

With the expanse of the roaring North Sea stretched before him Jon picked up the roundest pebble he could find and held it in his hand. It fitted his palm snugly and his other hand felt the roundness and contours of the stone. He examined it and held it up to the golden light eclipsing the sun. Then, without thought as if he were a child, he threw it into the foaming ocean where it fell with a dull splash, ripples melting into the waves.

Not really realising it Jon had moved the rock fifty metres, a journey that had taken eons through the constant action of the seas. In the lapping water it dropped gently to the bed and snuggled itself into the soft sand of its new home.

Jon turned and walked back to his car, already packed for his journey south. As he started the engine he looked back at the sea and vowed he would return.

Prague

October 1787

The streets of Prague were busy, teeming with people on a cold market day. Wolfgang Amadeus Mozart walked the narrow streets with a proud gait and occasionally someone would nod to acknowledge him.

The previous night his new opera Don Giovanni had premiered at the National Theatre to a wonderful reception. The audience had given him and his company a standing ovation. At last his father would be proud of him. Thirty-one years old, a man of limited but independent means and still he sought his stern parent's approval ! From now on it would be different.

He approached the Carolius Bridge, a grand and wide thoroughfare that snaked rakishly across the river where hawkers sold trinkets, flowers, pictures, fruit, themselves, indeed all manner of goods, anything to make a few coins. He looked at the pleading faces, wanting only what everyone yearned; security and a full belly.

He left the bridge walking under the tall gated towers which dominated each end and found himself in a small square facing the baroque church of Saint Francis. Something, perhaps fate, called him to enter and he pushed open the great carved oak door and took solace in the relative warmth of the marble interior. He was greeted by the priest who was just leaving confession.

"Good day to you sir !" the priest said offering a hand which Mozart shook vigorously.

"And to you Holy Father" Mozart replied, "the day is a little cold and God's house is a welcome relief"

"God protects in many ways does he not ?" The priest said in reply.

Mozart looked to the ceiling decorated with murals depicting the life of Saint Francis and his eye was caught by the organ. His heart missed a beat as his musician's instinct was electrified. "Holy Father, may I ask a favour ?" Mozart asked, his throat feeling dry in anticipation, "may I play your church organ ?"

The priest noticed the childlike excitement in Mozart's eyes. "Certainly sir ! How could I refuse !" And Mozart almost dashed up the stairs toward the keyboard.

He sat taking in the atmosphere for some moments. He smelt the incense. He felt the solemnity, peace and tranquillity of the building and the hope of those that had visited it. And he began to play. The keyboard bent to his will, as if the instrument had been made just for him.

The complex melody that came to him without thought or effort was simple but glorious. The sound of rumbling bass and soaring keys echoed around the great dome and the priest sat behind him enthralled. Mozart played note perfect and in his head choirs sang an angelic harmony to counterpoint the melody. It would be a perfect finale to a requiem.

With a majestic and grand flourish he ended the piece and the last notes reverberated around the nave seeking out every nook and cranny of the vast chamber. Mozart sighed in satisfaction thanking heaven for his talent.

As he rose and walked slowly down the stairs the priest spoke, "Wonderful ! Majestic ! Beautiful !" The priest said in praise. "You must write it down..." and the priest picked up a prayer book. "Come to my study sir. I have a pen and some ink. You must write it down."

There was no real need. Mozart knew the piece and could annotate the score perfectly when he arrived home. The priest, however, was insistent and Mozart followed him into the study where the priest and he sat for an hour talking and writing the many parts that echoed in Mozart's head, producing a full score in the back pages of an old prayer book.

Atlantic Ocean

15th April 1912

The night to remember had begun quietly. They had left the third class restaurant early in the evening and gone to their bunks but, at around 11:40 Eric and Katherine had been awakened by a loud explosion. The children slept soundly but Eric knew there was something wrong.

Within half an hour it became apparent that Titanic's short voyage was at an end, the berg they had hit had ripped a tear along the length of the vessel and she was fast taking in water. To the passengers' astonishment the captain had given the order to abandon ship.

On deck the new rocket flares were fired to signal a vessel on the horizon but there had been no recognition. Most chattered away or sat on deck chairs enjoying the excitement, convinced that rescue was only minutes away.

Eric felt differently. In the growing panic he decided to get his family on deck and find them a place in a lifeboat. With tenacity he managed to persuade one of the 2nd Class pursers to allow his wife and children into one of the boats that had a few spaces on it.

He wrapped the twins in blankets to stop them shivering in the cold night air. Before settling them in the boat he had hugged them tightly and knew in that moment he would never see them again. He kissed his sweet Katherine and reassured her. Once all the other women and children were safe he would find a space in another boat, after all most of those launched already had plenty of space, there would be room enough for all.

For the next half hour Eric looked after two young boys who had become separated from their family. He kept their spirits up and they planned an escape route. Suddenly the ship lurched violently and from where they stood they saw the stern lifting high out of the water. This was the time. He looked at his watch, it was 2:20. He scrambled to the hand rail holding the two frightened boys by the hand. He looked over the side and the long drop to the dark water below. He prayed that with the life jackets they would survive.

They climbed over the rail and immediately the ship jolted again and one of the boys fell to the water and disappeared. This was the moment and he jumped. Time slowed and it seemed an eternity to the water. As he went under he hadn't realised how ice cold it was going to be. His instincts took over and he swam for the surface, bobbed up and fought for breath.

"Christ it was cold ! Help us now. Lord help us now," and under his breath he chanted a prayer. It was in that moment, at the lonely second while swimming for his life that he realised he was going to die. He did not want to drown but he could feel the cold sap his strength and numb his muscles. His breath becoming shallower and struggling, he swam towards the noise of others in the water but the sounds were hushed.

In its death throws the ship finally broke in two, its stern high in water, a black tombstone in the night and it sank majestically into the darkness until the fires of the funnels could be seen orange as they disappeared under the surface. The pride of the White Star was gone.

As Eric watched it disappear he thought of his lost life, his lost opportunities, his lost love, his lost family and he wept as he shivered. He felt a pang of regret and betrayal. Cheated. Around him in the tragic cold ocean many miles from land and safety 1523 lives felt the same betrayal. The cold was stealing every drop of his life's blood but still he found the strength to weep . He cried to the wind and the seas that tossed him like a feather and screamed into the darkness of the night and the glow of the dawn breaking in the East. His last lonely cry was ignored.

"I am not ready, " he cried, "I am not ready ! Lord have mercy !" Slowly the bitter cold of the sea numbed his body and slowed his heart and with the sound of music ringing in his ears Eric died. The sea washed around his limp body as the moon shone and rippled on the water. Men come and go and the tide turns once more.

Chapter 5

Opening Moves

"We have learnt that for each life a death must be endured to maintain the equilibrium. We know that the departed will not rest until balance is restored and justice is served."

Jarrat Toldon, Chronicles of the Future

"How can you fight the fire when you're fuelling the flames?"

Neil Peart

London

The Present

*I*t was a dark voice. A voice of malice. A voice of perversion. A voice from one's darkest nightmare. An evil voice.

"You know your purpose. You have done well for me. Do this again. I thirst. I hunger. More time can be yours."

Ranulf was ageless. His life of four centuries lived in a body of only 35 years. In his time he had seen so much and he knew what his dark Lord meant. More time on this earth. A reward for more souls. More murder, more misdirection, more lost souls. He knew he was well in credit.

He had *been* for so long and had seen so much he had become a hardened cynic. He knew it to be true. The years of cynicism blunts away the freshness of life. With every extra day another load is laid across the shoulders like a heavy burden. It weighs so heavy it twists your mind until you believe in nothing and in no one.

Ranulf had one vision to which he was true to. One mission. His mission was easy. Locate the victims soon after death as they drift into the waiting time and into the next life. Lead them *into temptation* toward the false gateway then lead them through it. That there should be such a mistake in the fabric of creation was incredible to him.

Disasters were his favoured location. It was so easy to misguide when they meet an end too soon and had drifted into the wait state. They were like sheep following each other toward a false oblivion.

In reward his was given more time and more life; his commission. How many could there have been. Thousands perhaps ? He was sure his dark Lord knew, anyway it was not his problem. Do what everyone else does through their pitiful lives. Do the job, ask no questions and snatch at the rewards.

He often wondered if the gatekeepers of paradise knew. Surely they knew souls were missing. Perhaps they had never realised that the numbers were out. Perhaps they would never know.

He had often pondered on the interesting theory that tries to bring order from chaos. That, for example, the slightest action in one place can causing perhaps a violent reaction in another. He had realised this was also true of time. If fate is really laid out for everyone even before our lives begin imagine the effects of a man dying before his time. Untimely death causing ripples down through the decades. The question is. Could anyone map those causes and effects ?

On earth he had become a collector, a gatherer of objects, of the rare and beautiful. Twenty years before, some of his possessions had been ripped from his sanctuary, why, he knew not, but he would have them back - they would be returned to him.

For now he waited. In his opinion a fallen angel had more pleasures and he willingly drowned in the hedonism of sex and drugs and perversion. A demon on earth - what an assignment.

And he concentrated on his next, "...who is to be intercepted this time ? Some poor unfortunate..." and he glowed as he thought of it.

Ranulf felt the rush of possession as his master injected him with the power for his next mission. He felt his nerve ends tingle and his senses sharpen and prepared himself for the journey into dreamtime.

"Ranulf, " his master said, "...you must be wary, you must be alert. There are those who would stop your theft and deception. Be on your guard !"

Ranulf felt the energy coursing through his body, "...I am always on my guard master. Your tasks are my eternal pleasure. I will bring you more souls to feed upon. I will revel in your triumphs..." Ranulf replied in joy.

And with that his journey began. He was now travelling into coldness through pain, hurtling past visions and lost lifetimes toward the gateway. It was an icy cold and soulless place, he abhorred it yet he lusted for it. Lust, the pleasure his work gave him. And his surroundings changed. A speck of white light flickered in the distance. A spirit had begun their journey.

Isle of Lewis

August 1477

It had been a rough sailing but they had survived the currents, tempest and storms of the Caledonian coast. On its journey the tiny "Spirit" had been sheltered by Ireland to the West and Scotland to the East. They had now sailed to the Hebrides to take on fresh water and food for the journey to Iceland. If they were lucky the crossing to Vinland would be ice free and calm. If they were lucky.

Njal, the coxswain, had not been lucky. They had sailed into Uig bay and been taking on fresh barrels of water. One of the barrels had broken free and had crushed his ribcage puncturing a lung. In his bunk and in great pain Njal was dying.

Christoph and Bartholemo had made great friends with Njal. He had told them sagas and tales of the New Lands. Of the journey of Erikson where he found a land of strange men and where vines grew on the gentle slopes. The sagas of Vorland to lands of hot sun and strange mounds where the men of the land buried their noble dead.

The captain had been a reserved and quiet man, obviously suspicious of the brothers' mission however their friendship had grown with Njal and he had even taught them a game with two miniature armies that was played with bone and ivory pieces.

Njal had three sets that, he told them, were handed down to him by his father and grandfather and were some three hundred years old. Some of the pieces were missing but two full sets survived. Many times during their games Christoph had been distracted by the beautifully carved whale bone and walrus tusk.

Njal told them of how there were many on Vinland who had given up the dangerous job of sailing to farm the cold Vinland fields. Life was hard but secure. Far away from the politics and intrigue of the new Danish king.

In the darkness of the long winter nights they kept the stories and sagas alive keeping warm around log fires. Some had even settled in what they called the New Lands and exported vegetables, produce and timber and built ships and settlements.

Christoph and Bartholemo sat in silence next to Njal's bunk and watched as he faded in and out of consciousness. Occasionally he stirred and moaned in pain.

Then Njal took a slow and agonising breath. "You must build a pyre and scatter my ashes..." he said wincing, his voice almost inaudible.

Christoph held the man's blood caked hand and squeezed it. "I promise" he said, affirming his friend's request.

"Bury my sets. I will need something to play in Valhalla," and he smiled. He opened his eyes enough to see Christoph. "I hope you will one day see our New World."

Then, Njal looked from his bed through the open window towards the fading light and watched the sunset for his last time and died.

Bartholemo wept as they helped to wrap Njal's body in hessian and sail cloth. Early the next day they rowed ashore to a shallow sandy inlet and built a pyre fit for a God.

They lit the kindling and watched the flames enveloped the body standing in solemnity and reverence as the body burnt.

An hour later they sat warming themselves by the fire as it died and told tales of their childhood and homelands.

In the evening they scattered the cool ashes and decided to bury the sets as Njal had requested, choosing the shelter of an ancient ruined watchtower.

Just as he was about to lower the stitched leather bag into the shallow hole they had dug in the sand, Christoph dipped into the bag pulling out one of the finest pieces, carved in walrus tusk which he identified as one of the kings. It wore a crown, clutched a sword across its lap and frowned solemnly, perhaps disapprovingly at him. The throne on which it sat was intricately carved with Celtic twists and patterns interwoven with tiny dragons and griffins. It was a beautifully carved piece and he placed it in the pocket of his breeches as a keepsake of their friendship.

Out in the bay they heard the ship's bell on the *Spirit* summoning them back to the ship and they reluctantly rowed back to continue their mission.

As the *Spirit* sailed away, Christoph and Bartholemo watched from the foredeck as the lands of their ancestors disappeared on the horizon and they bid their friend farewell.

* * * * *

40

Later that evening Jon arrived in Edinburgh and checked into a hotel close to the castle and Royal Mile. After a light dinner he took a walk down into Prince's Street to settle himself for the night. The breeze funnelled down the long street blowing like a wind tunnel chilling his face and after only half an hour he returned to the hotel for an early night. Perhaps it would be warmer in the morning and he could spend a few hours exploring the city.

His room was spacious and comfortable and the soft bed seemed to envelop him. He fell asleep immediately and dreamt of his brother.

"...Jon..its me...I think we've discovered the problem...." His brother's voice seemed bright and crisp.

Jon recognised the voice but struggled to reply, "Daniel...what is it...?"

"We think someone's masquerading as a spirit guide..." Daniel said. Daniel explained about the moment of death when you enter a short period of limbo where a decision is made as to your next assignment. Usually this takes just a few moments - you are either sent to a debriefing, sent to rest or returned immediately to your next host.

"It is our belief that souls are being taken within the wait state." Daniel concluded.

"Surely you can see who that person is ?"

"Well, we could normally. There have been isolated cases where a medium or psychic has accidentally misguided souls during the period but this is resolved with the soul being returned to themselves - what people believe to be out of body experiences. In this case, however, we have searched and drawn a blank. If he or she was a rogue psychic or a medium we would have found them. We've come to the belief that the misguider is not of earth and therefore not obligated to heaven."

"You're talking about a darker side aren't you ?"

There was a silence as Daniel considered a diplomatic reply but could think of none, "Yes Jon. I'm afraid I am......It could have been going on for centuries. But they appear to be increasing in frequency. If these souls are being sent to the dark world who ever holds them has an increasing army. There are souls who should not be doomed for eternity for living good lives. It cannot be tolerated."

"...Surely this has caused some sort of imbalance...", Jon asked.

"The more that disappear the more reassignments have to be undertaken. Some have to stay within the wait state until a suitable host is found. I am one of them. The longer I stay within the wait state the more chance I have of being returned to an unsuitable host. Returning to learn lessons which are already learned and not following planned destinies."

"...Surely there are forces working which I have no power to combat ?"

"Jon. We know you believe in the eternal soul. The life force without ending which cannot be created, merely reborn. We also know you believe in deduction by logic without guesswork. This is all we seek from you Jon."

There was such confidence in the voice Jon could not question it. He felt himself pushed back into a deep sleep with gentle but immense force and he slept peacefully once more.

The next morning he woke refreshed and ate breakfast in the hotel restaurant. He wrapped up well in his thick warm and windproof coat and walked into the already busy Princes Street. He browsed through a couple of music stores and found an old Vangelis album for which he'd been searching, "Spiral". In tiny script he read the Tao proverb on the cover - '...Going on mean going far, Going far means returning...' It somehow seemed appropriate to the moment. He paid the assistant and popped the CD in his deep pocket to play in the car.

Edinburgh was at its busiest. It was the last week of festival month and every corner had a busker or someone passing you a leaflet for one show or another. Three years before he had spent a week with his wife doing the fringe and festival and they had a wonderful time. So much to do and so very little time to do it. He smiled at the memory of it.

Eventually he found himself in the National Museum of Scotland and after browsing the paintings decided to look around the ancient Celtic artefacts, Pictish stones and the Norse brooches. One particular set of objects caught his eye. It was a set of ivory chess pieces - the famous Lewis Chess set found in the spring of 1831 in Uig Bay on the west coast of Lewis in the Outer Hebrides. How they had got there was a mystery. The set had been made at about 1180 somewhere in Scandinavia. They were magnificent examples of the craftsmen's skill and Jon viewed them through the glass from every angle.

Each piece was intricately carved, even the throne on which the queen sat was knotted with Celtic twists. The faces on each piece looked so serious and grim but he especially liked the knights who were seated on stocky shaggy fringed Icelandic ponies. Some eighty pieces had been found, most of which were in the British Museum in London, but these, Jon felt, were somehow special. There were almost two complete sets but curiously the king from one of the sets was missing.

Vienna

May 1972

Zetler was in his early fifties with a thick swept back mane of white hair. He was a happy man who bubbled with energy. He had a bright moon face with large brown eyes which twinkled with the knowledge and experience of his life. His house on the edge of Vienna overlooking the Wienerwald was compact and full of memories and bric-a-brac he had collected over the years.

He laid the aluminium case on the kitchen table and excitedly opened it. Inside were a number of packages and he carefully removed each one. The first was nearly a metre long and he carefully unwrapped the large bulbous end revealing the gleaming pommel of a sword. He rewrapped it and placed it on one side for Hirschfelden in Salzburg.

The next was a small brown paper parcel containing a small bound volume. He removed the paper revealing a small black prayer book with music written into the back cover. He would send it on to West Germany.

A roll of parchment wrapped tightly with a faded ribbon. He removed the ribbon, which disintegrated and the parchment unrolled itself. The faded drawings were instantly recognisable as sketches from the notebooks of Da Vinci. The museum of the Prado would be more than happy with the prize.

Giggling, like a small boy on Christmas morning he took the next, not knowing what he would find. He removed the paper and took out the thick volume inside it. He gently turned the sepia pages and giggled with delight.

The volume was a first folio print of William Shakespeare and John Fletcher's lost collaborations. It contained the completed "Tragedy of Mary Queen of Scots" and the incomplete "History of the Discovery of the New World" by both Shakespeare and Fletcher. The third was the play "Hamlet and Gertrude" by Shakespeare alone which, from first glance, seemed to be a romance in the style of "Romeo and Juliet" and a prequel to "Hamlet, Prince of Denmark". Zetler chuckled with delight. This was to be a gift for the British Library in London.

Zetler opened a small box containing an engraved cigarette case of little intrinsic value but of import for the future. He tucked it in a pocket for safety.

Zetler marvelled at the objects before him and the drive of Ranulf collecting them. His priority now was to disperse them as quickly as possible to their rightful owners and ensure they were secure in their new homes. He went upstairs to pack for the journey and as he did so he pondered on the necessity of the crime but his conscience did not dwell on it. He knew it could have not been accomplished without the help of the brotherhood.

Dallas, Texas

22nd November 1963

Bob and Jennie had taken time off work and stood excitedly on the corner of Elm waiting for the President's cavalcade to arrive. If it were slow enough they would get a glimpse of the President and Jackie. Bob held his little Kodak ready to maybe snap a few photographs.

The sun was bright and warmed their shoulders and they both shaded their eyes from the burning Texas sun light. They could hear the distant cheering as the motorcade got closer.

Everyone cheered for the President and Jackie. He was a good President, he had given them a sense of national pride and they were the perfect couple.

Bob stood on tip toe and made out the leading police motorcyclists ahead of the open topped limo. The car had turned the corner and they waved and shouted frantically.

"JFK JFK..." they shouted and waved and cheered.

And the scene changed into slo-mo......

Three shots broke the silence of the dream.

Bang.....   One from behind them...

Crack

Bang.....   One from the knoll in front of them...

Bang.....   And one from the bridge....

Bob instinctively pushed Jennie onto the ground for cover and they looked up in horror as they saw JFK's body slumped against Jackie. Lifeless.

The black car sped quickly out of sight under the bridge.

Horror and disbelief sank into the now stunned onlookers. Bob and Jennie and the thousands that watched stood in silence and shock, time standing still.

The dream had ended. He was gone. It was all over. No future, just painful memories.

Too young. Too early. Too soon.

Chapter 6

Onward into Darkness

"We will each take many voyages and visit many ports of call believing we sail on charted oceans steering a steady course. But, how we drift aimlessly on the tide often reaching our destinations not by judgement but by luck. Arriving on the distant shore as a sailor on the seas of fate."

> Jarrat Toldon, Chronicles of the Future

"Head into the headlight, don't turn from the rain."

> Yes

*J*on had enjoyed his day in Edinburgh exploring its nooks and crannies. The impressive Georgian facades of New Town contrasted with the narrow wynds and closes of Old Town had charmed him. He knew he was destined to return there.

Some hours later he was driving south on the M74 toward the borders where the countryside was a little monotonous. He passed the small town of Lockerbie and remembered the evening in December 1988 when he had heard the news flash that bought the devastating news of the crash of Pan Am flight 101.

By mid afternoon he was driving past the hills of the Lake District with the Langdales rising on the western horizon and worked out he would make Birmingham by about seven in the evening in time to freshen up and enjoy a good Chinese meal.

He always found driving an escape and enjoyed the freedom and flexibility of it. His car, a 1986 silver Opel Monza and feminine character, was quite a rarity but still had the power to cruise effortlessly. The car hugged the black tarmac and Jon's challenges and responsibilities became a blur as he concentrated on the road.

He eased the car into the middle lane and slowed for the worsening weather. Approaching Manchester the rain lashed the windscreen like stair rods reducing visibility further and the rain zigzagged down the side windows. Behind him a BMW flashed for him to move over, impatient in spite of the conditions.

After stopping for coffee and refilling the car with petrol he returned to the motorway and switched on the CD player. After a few moments every corner of the car was bathed with sound.

Music was a drug to which he was addicted and he relished it. It had the power to raise the spirits and spark the senses.

The CD player selected tracks at random. It chose a piece by Swiss harpist Andreas Vollenweider from "Down to the Moon" then a track from Vangelis' "Direct".

A piece of atmospheric Celtic harp by Alan Stivell whirred into the machine. Then a strange rush whispered through the speakers and the music faded out and dissolved into hiss and static.

Jon looked at the player checking the device hadn't developed a fault. "Probably a speck of dust on the head," he thought.

And then pushing through the static came the voices.

"Release us," they whispered, "help us," they pleaded, "take us home," they begged. The sad, ethereal voices faded away.

Jon stared at the machine then into the rear view mirror, then to the dotted white line of the road disappearing under the bonnet of the car.

The music returned to the sprightly lilt of the harp.

He was sweating. For those seconds the car had been driving itself.

* * * * *

Annelise had spent the evening in a local *stube* with friends but had not discussed her dreams. That night she slept well and her dreams began immediately, she hoped her love would come to her and was not disappointed. Through a mist and haze came his voice.

"Sweet Annelise ! It is me, my love." Reinhardt greeted her with a warm embrace.

"Reinhardt," she whispered softly feeling the warmth of love in her breast.

"Annie, I have a gift for you ! You will receive it tomorrow," there was teasing in the voice.

46

"A gift ? From you ? What is it ?" Annelise said excitedly.

"No my love. You must be patient. You will see it tomorrow. Now sleep my darling," and with the comforting voice in her head Annelise lapsed into a deep dreamless sleep.

The next morning Annelise over slept. Once awake she pulled back the duvet and wrapped a silk dressing gown around herself rushing down to the postkasten to see if her dream was true. In it was a small parcel addressed in Reinhardt's hand but with a post mark that indicated it was posted in Stuttgart the day before. There was also the return post sticker of one of the well-established solicitors in the city.

She carefully unwrapped it, breaking the brittle sealing wax. Inside was a battered and old prayer book and from the German gothic text she guessed it was probably about two hundred years old. Inside was a note dated 23rd November 1943. It was from Reinhardt. It read :

Herrenberg   23rd November 1943

My Love,

By the time you read this note I shall have been gone fifty years but I know you will have not forgotten me. I knew when we parted last night we would not see each other in this life time again. I therefore enclose this gift knowing how you love Mozart. It took some time to find it for you after I was told it existed. One day we will meet again. Until then.

For Now My Love.

Reinhardt

Annelise turned carefully through the sepia pages and could not understand the reference to Mozart.

She reached the faded back pages of the book. The final four sheets, normally blank, were covered with music scratched in black ink. It looked hastily scribbled in a moment of inspiration. There were a few mathematical equations doodled in the margins.

It was titled "Glorianna" and there were two simple initials below it.

They were W.A.

North West Atlantic Ocean

September 1985

Jason was a good name for a questor, an apt title for one who seeks. Jason was a small remote control research submarine and its search was nearing an end. It had been scanning the depths for signs of a ship that had lain in the mud for over 75 years. For weeks its hunt had been fruitless.

Many days, many hours, many lost sleepless nights and thousands of dollars had been ploughed into what some described as desecration but others saw as one of the last great adventures. For the expedition leader it was an obsession.

Jason's silicon brain knew it was close, it could almost smell the great wreck and could feel it's magnetic pull. Suddenly as the search beams cut the darkness the brightness hit a wall and voices on the surface became excited. Jason's engines cut for an instant and it slowly rose, the search light beams tracing the bulk and what was the bow of a great vessel unseen since 1912.

As Jason rose to deck level the identity was unambiguous. It was the rusting hulk of the "Titanic" magnificent in the darkness. On the surface voices cheered and shouted with satisfaction, their quest complete. Against all the odds and misinformation they had found the "Titanic".

Jason moved along the rotting deck to the empty and ghostly wheel house. Search lights shone through open port holes and down broken and twisted stairwells. At the centre of the vessel the stern was missing. The ship had broken in two and the stern was a few hundred yards away.

Jason was bought down to skim the sea bed and its fans threw wisps of mud and sand into the water. Suddenly as the beams cut the darkness of the ocean bed the light caught glints of metal. Jason sailed through the flotsam and jetsam of mankind two miles beneath the ocean; a buckle on a shoe, a length of ladder, a doll, a rusty hand rail, a bed head; a graveyard of objects.

Something else sparkled in the mirk and Jason's beams zoomed in on it. It was a silver cigarette case sitting on a window frame, the glass still intact. Jason reached out a robotic hand to examine the find. With gentle mechanical dexterity it picked up the slim box and held it between metal claws. The case was in perfect condition and the lid bore a scrolled engraving bold and clear across the top right corner.

E. M.

* * * * *

Jon arrived in Birmingham a little after seven and checked into a central hotel close to the city centre and night life. The city had changed much. For years, Jon had worked in one of its shining ivory towers. He had seen many a sunrise flower in corals and reds over the city. From the top of one of the high tower office blocks on a clear morning you felt you could see for ever.

As he planned, after freshening up, Jon took a taxi to his favourite Cantonese restaurant, Chung Dynasty close to the Hippodrome Theatre. He chose a quiet table and was handed the menu. He was very hungry and his mouth watered at the thought of Cantonese spare ribs.

After making his choice he looked up from his menu and there across the restaurant seated at the bar was one of the most beautiful women he had every seen. He was captivated by her. She had bright green eyes and her dark chestnut hair shone like silk. She was aware of his gaze.

He could feel her presence from across the room. She glanced up from her drink and smiled at him.

There was a strange electricity between them. Something drew him to her. Without thinking he decided to ask if she wanted to join him. He approached and stood awkwardly behind her.

He took a breath . "I know this sounds crazy, " she turned around from the bar and gazed at him. She seemed to look into his soul. Her perfume washed over and drowned him and he felt himself glow.

"I don't want you to take this wrong, and I know we've only just noticed each other, but..." he realised he was stumbling over the words.

"Yes ?" She said laconically, amused at his embarrassment.

"Would you like to join me ?" he asked.

She thanked him with a smile and he showed her to his table.

The meal was perfect, the wine heady and they enjoyed each other's laughter and company. It was peculiar, but her manner and what she said made Jon feel that they had known each other before but, there was also something he sensed in her eyes of sadness and sorrow. He looked across the table at her.

She sat calmly, looking back at him, the hint of a smile on her rouge lips. Her black dress shimmered in the candlelight, her hands rested on the arms of the carver chair. The dark wood of the chair contrasting with her alabaster skin. The candles flickered in her green eyes warm but piercing.

"You don't know me do you ?" She asked.

"No, but I feel we have met." He replied.

She nodded, "I know what you want to ask. There is no one. I have never loved. I can never love..."

Jon's heart went out to her. He wanted to hold her. Comfort her. Love her. He desired her, "what do you mean ?" He asked.

"Once I would have loved. Once I would have given everything for a life of peace and warmth but now I have a different path. I am not as you think."

Jon frowned, perplexed by her words.

"I have a mission. I am bitter and twisted. I am vengeful. I am Nemesis. I am now Death's Mistress. You must be careful. You must forget me," and emotionally she rose from the table.

"But wait," Jon said reaching out to take her hand, "Why are you here ?"

"Forget me !" She said turning accusingly toward him.

With this she hurried across the restaurant picked up her coat and clutch bag and ran through the door and into the street.

Stunned at first, he followed close behind her. In the street he looked up and down the quiet thoroughfare.

She had vanished.

He sighed in frustration and in his head, perhaps in guilt, perhaps in memory he could hear his wife playing the piano and Beethoven's Fur Elise echoed in his thoughts.

Chapter 7

Guardian of Truth

"For many the earth turns slowly, each day melting into the last and the next with life a monotonous drudgery of eat, sleep, work but, this is the path they have chosen. For a few, the movers and shakers, they shape and mould their destinies. Their fate may not be altered but the path they have chosen is an enlightened highway with twists, turns and vision."

Jarrat Toldon, Chronicles of the Future

"Focus is hard in the city."

Neil Peart

With the smell of her perfume on his skin and the thought of her warmth Jon lapsed into slumber. He would dream again tonight. As he expected the voices came.

"Jon. She was beautiful !" Daniel said.

"You saw ? You can see things from where you are ?"

"Well I do have a special status for a short while," Daniel hesitated "You see Jon I am, for now, I'm a channel of your guardian angel. Everyone has one."

Jon was a little surprised, "Does this mean you keep me out of trouble ?"

"You angel has already ! Remember last winter, you sent your car into a skid. You fought with the wheel until the situation was worse than ever, until you let go the wheel. The car slowed its course and came to a gentle stop."

"I always thought that was weird !"

"Well, I will try to warn you if disaster is about to strike but will not always be able get you out of it. Thought I don't see why I should, you haven't even visited my marker yet !"

"Ah yes. You're right," Jon spluttered in embarrassment, "I guess I could go tomorrow." Jon thought for a moment, "you know Daniel, it's sort of comforting knowing someone cares." Jon's mind wandered back to the mission, "Daniel, have you any more information about the spirit thief ?"

"We're putting the pieces together here, but it is difficult. We know fragments of the jig-saw but making any sense of it is a challenge. We also believe we're running out of time."

Jon could see a significance in his brothers' comments, "what exactly do you mean ?"

"Well, when you're born you're granted a fixed number of days to complete an assignment - your allotted time. If for some reason you leave before that time you spend the remaining time within the wait state, unless a surrogate host can be found or until your next mission is assigned. This happened to me and I've been given this task until my time is done. It is only for a short while, and they thought, I was suited to the role."

"It sounds like a deadline to me."

"Yes Jon. Is it. There are those who can not rest until it is done. They will not rest..." and Daniel's voice faded again into the darkness.

The next day Jon decided to relieve the pangs of guilt by putting some flowers on his brother's grave. He also decided he would visit one of the exhibitions that had caught his eye while he was in the city. He thought about trying to trace the woman at the restaurant, but he suspected it would be a fruitless search. Somehow he had a strange feeling they would meet again.

The drive to Wolverhampton, his home town, was a bleak one, a journey through streets of terraced houses, factories, red brick smoke stacks and derelict wastelands. Jon had, however, grown to love the Black Country as it was called and its friendly, approachable people.

Climbing over Sedgley Bank at night you could see lights and life to the farthest horizon. It wasn't much to look at by day but by night it was like a cityscape lifted from a Ridley Scott movie. Once through Sedgley he turned off the main roads over the common to Penn Church where his brother's ashes were buried in the churchyard.

He had bought just a few red and white carnations and hoped they would be enough to brighten the grave up. The stone was set in a chess board of others, slotted in to save space so close you had to tread on other stones to get to the flower urn. It seemed strangely anonymous.

He removed the few dead heads from his last visit and replaced them with the new blooms. He had a few left over and popped one or two in neighbouring vases. He dusted the moss from the stone with an old newspaper and stood up to see his handiwork.

Would this be all there was left of him when he departed this earth ? It seemed so little to be left after a life time and he stood looking down at the plane stone containing only a name and a set of dates. He felt a twinge of bitterness, mingled with sadness. He looked up to the skies and cold raindrops patted his face. He had been so lost in his thoughts that he hadn't noticed it had begun to gently rain.

Jon drove back to Birmingham with the heater on to dry his clothes and hair. The traffic had built up since early in the morning with business men out on their break. Pub car parks were full and office car parks were empty. The British at their most industrious !

He parked back at the hotel and decided to across the inner ring road to the Museum and Art Gallery. He paid a regular pilgrimage to the art gallery to visit the Pre-Raphaelite collection which he particularly enjoyed. It also had romantic connections as this was were he used to meet his wife at lunch time when they had first met. He smiled to himself as he named the pictures he knew so well; "Boer War", "Last of England" , "Death of Chatterton" such a romantic time.

He stayed for over an hour, sitting to take in the peace and richness of the room. He then walked to the other side of the building to a special touring exhibition that was almost at the end of it's three month visit.

The exhibition was titled "Treasures of the Titanic" and contain artefacts recovered from the SS Titanic in various missions since she was rediscovered in September 1985.

The pieces were fascinating, each with their own story; a tale of parting, a tale of loss and a tale of sadness. In the display case before him he saw a leather shoe, a brass bed head, a ladder, a doll and a silver cigarette box.

It was this last piece that caught his eye. It was engraved with the initials :

E. M.

He read the card beneath it.

Even before restoration this silver engraved cigarette case had survived well after over 70 years on the ocean floor.

It belonged to a 30 year old Irish doctor, Eric Matheson who came from Knocklinn south of Dublin and who was on his way to Chicago to start a new life with his wife and two daughters.

His wife and children luckily survived the sinking after being rescued by the Carpathia some hours later. His daughter now aged 87 lives in North Carolina told researchers how they last saw their father a few yards from their life boat. A line was thrown from the boat but before he could be reached he sank beneath the waves. Dr Eric Matheson is still listed as missing presumed dead.

Jon returned to his hotel very much affected by what he had seen. He had noted down everything he had read but didn't know quite why just that he should.

The story of Eric and his lost years reminded him of those of his brother but it seemed strange that Eric was so close to a lifeboat and was not saved. He must have heard the sounds of his wife and daughters calling to him. It just seemed incomprehensible that moments from safety he could give up.

There was so many unanswered questions to the case he decided that he wanted to contact Eric, if that were possible through his brother. He would try it when next in dream state.

He tucked the notes into his pocket and decided to take a walk around the city centre and find a restaurant. Tomorrow he would continue his journey but his destination was still a mystery to him.

Yosemite National Park, California

The drive to Yosemite from San Francisco was short and offered few highlights. Drew stopped close outside Manceta at a roadhouse for a coffee and a piece of delicious banana creme pie. He ate it quickly and pressed on, his aim to be in the park before nightfall and find a room.

Trees were just beginning to turn to their autumnal shades of brown, russet and gold. The park was still quite busy; climbers scaled El Capitan and there were still plenty of hikers and cyclist on the trails, but then Yosemite was rarely quiet.

He arrived at the central park office and was surprised to find a room booked for him in the Sequoia Lodge hotel. A message awaited him asking him to meet Jeremiah Monday at the ranger station at ten the next day. Evidently someone knew more about this trip than he did !

The next morning Drew had a light breakfast and walked the short distance from the hotel to the ranger station. He asked to meet Mr Monday and was handed a coffee and shown into a windowless functional office with two chairs and a desk.

After some minutes the door opened, "good morning Drew ! Glad you could make it. My name's Jeremiah Monday."

Before him was a Native American Indian, probably in his early sixties. Jeremiah wore jeans, a lumberjack shirt and gold rimmed glasses. Around his wrist he wore a delicate turquoise bracelet. His eyes were dark and intense and wrinkles around his cheeks suggesting a cheery disposition.

"Good to meet you, " Drew said, "though I don't understand quite why we're here."

"There are many mysteries aren't there Drew," Jeremiah said enigmatically. "The more we find, there more there is yet to find !" Jeremiah sat down and began very efficiently. "Drew, I'm told you want to know something about early American history. Let me ask you a simple question. Who discovered America ?"

Drew hesitated for a moment expecting a trap in his question, "well, Christopher Columbus - you know." He continued, "in 14 Hundred and 92 Columbus sailed the ocean blue." reciting the old rhyme.

"Well. Yes. I did think you'd say that. What would you say if I told you you were wrong. What would you say if I told you the New World was discovered, if that is the right expression, some four centuries earlier by the Vikings ?"

"I guess I'd be surprised and ask what the evidence was," Drew said sceptically.

"There is plenty of evidence, certainly on the east coast. A number of settlements have been found around Newfoundland where the Vikings crossed the perilous straight from Greenland in search of whale. At the time, around 950AD the Viking settlers met the Indians and there was an exchange of cultures. There was respect between the two different civilisations."

While speaking Jeremiah had been toying with a small cardboard box that he now placed in the centre of the table.

"The Vikings were present in what they called Vinland for many years until most of them either died or returned to the safety of the Danish nation. At that time they didn't realise they had left behind their diseases that spread like wildfire. They visited this land not realising what the effects could be." Drew detected a hint of sadness in the old man's voice.

While he spoke Jeremiah tapped the top of the box with a tanned finger.

"This is one of the reasons I live and work in Yosemite. I'm a cultural historian. I'm actually based at Berkeley when the weather turns bad up here. In the hills we recently found the burial chamber of a Lakota chief. The first thing we noticed was that the chief was interred in something resembling a Norse burial chamber. He was buried with all the usual riches for his journey to the next world, as the ancient Egyptians would have been buried. One of the items found with him was this."

Jeremiah carefully lifted the lid of the small cardboard box. Inside it was packed with cotton wool protecting a small object some four inches high. Unwrapping it Jeremiah revealed an intricately carved ivory figure about three inches high and moulded like a king.

Jeremiah held the piece up to the florescent light examining its art work from every angle. "Do you play chess Drew ?" He asked.

Vienna

December 1791

The light of the day was fading and Mozart felt weak. The drugs which he had been prescribed dulled the pain but he felt weak. In his heart he felt angry. He knew that his time was short but he also knew he still had much to do.

His head was full of a new symphony, an opera based on the Shakespeare play Hamlet, a concerto for clarinet and he desperately wanted to finish his requiem. The piece he had written in Prague would be perfect for the finale - a majestic Glorianna.

His body was paralysed by the drugs and his breathing was shallow. He could just feel the hand of his beloved Constanze and the quiet sobs of his children. Deep down he suspected they would be better off without him.

He was, after all, a failure. They had little money, even the crowns that had paid for his drugs had been borrowed. He knew what he had done was right and that he would be remembered for his talent. His epitaph would be his music.

He felt another streak of pain course through his body. He gritted his teeth and his clutched his wife's hand tightly. In his other hand he squeezed the prayer book that he cherished with such fond memories.

Then, his mind cleared and he could hear such divine music in his head. Such beautiful music. It was his Glorianna.

Mozart took a last breath and with the sound of the Requiem Mass ringing in his ears he died.

* * * * *

Vinland

Summer of 1488

The journey from Greenland to the old Viking settlements of Vinland had been hazardous. The ship and its crew had survived only because of the skill and tenacity of the ship's master John Jay. Christoph and Barthelemo had rarely experienced sailing in the cold cruel waters of the North and they were now glad to see land.

They had been told that there was fresh water and sometimes fruit and corn to be found close to the banks of the wide river that they were navigating. On occasions the ship looked as if it would run aground and it was only the quick thinking of the helmsman that averted a disaster. Soon they were close to their chosen landing and they dropped anchor. A foraging party of eight was formed and as the brothers had volunteered they were included.

They rowed steadily toward a small beach. Soon they felt shingle scrape the keel of the boat and they stepped ashore.

A few yards from the water a line of trees hid the land beyond. To their surprise they could see a small face peering in curiosity at them from behind a tree. It didn't seem at all frightened but its eyes were bright with wonder like a cat. The eyes belonged to a nine year boy who was dress in buck skin breeches and had dirty bare feet. At his side he carried a short spear, which doubled as a fishing rod - three large trout were tied to the end of it.

Christoph told the crew to stay with the boat for safety and so that they would not alarm the boy. He approached the boy who stood his ground and showed no fear. He decided he needed to offer him something as a gift of friendship. His hand was at his side and he could feel the chess piece from Njal in his coat pocket. Slowly he took it out and kneeling down a few yards from the boy Christoph offered it to him.

Gingerly the boy took the piece and examined it. He held it to the light and smelt it. He felt it with his rough dirty hands and finally put it into his mouth to taste it. He then looked at the glum face of the king seated in his throne and chuckled. He pointed to the small figure and he laughed. Columbus smiled and laughed too.

There, on that quiet beach, was the one of the first meetings of the New and Old World civilisations. The meeting had been with smiles and trust. Sadly in the years to come it would not always be so.

Chapter 8

Revenge on the Weak

"Some are twisted by the present, others by the past and others by past lives. But a past life once completed is uncorrectable and offers no retake. It is true for those who must move further up the ladder and for those who must descend before they climb."

Jarrat Toldon, Chronicles of the Future

"The mirror always lies. Paint it black !"

Neil Peart

*T*hat night Jon went to bed early, having had no inspiration for his next destination from his stroll around the city. As he walked through the electric sliding doors into the warmth of the hotel foyer he looked back at the gleaming bright towers of the city. He was fond of Birmingham and would miss it. In his hotel room he looked across the metropolis toward the Rotunda, nicknamed the Coke Can by the locals, from the Coca Cola logo wrapped around its roof-top.

He closed the curtains and packed his commodious overnight bag for an early start, he felt that London should be his next move and felt that a reason would become apparent; it had thus far.

With the hum of the traffic still in his head he climbed into bed and closed his eyes. His thoughts turned to how lonely and soulless the city could be especially for the mystic or the dreamer and soon he was drifting into his own dream state and the voices came...

"Jon ! It's me again. I think we have a link for you," the voice said excitedly, we want you to visit Dorset, there are a few loose ends there you may help to tie up."

"Dorset ? We used to holiday there as children !"

"Yes, I remember. I'm told that you may find pointers there. We think you need to go to southwards anyway..."

"I've had an idea as well, can you talk to someone for me. His name is Dr Eric Matheson he was an Irish doctor who died on the Titanic. His wife and daughters were saved. I want to ask him a few questions if its possible."

Daniel thought for a moment, "well I'll ask. I don't see why there should be a problem. Why do you want to talk to him ?"

"Simple. I read an account of his death written by his daughter. He was so close to being rescued and seemed to just give up. It could have been exhaustion but, well, I'm just curious that's all."

"Okay Jon I'll see what I can do. Meanwhile, I'll visit tomorrow. Sweet dreams big brother !" And the voice dissolved into the night like a fading distant light.

The next day, after a short four hour journey, Jon arrived in the small market town of Wareham and checked into the expensive but luxurious Priory Hotel. He chose a small room, The Arne, that overlooked the manicured lawn and well kept gardens on the riverbank.

The town was quiet and had returned to normal after a busy summer. Most of the boats had been taken from the river for the winter but for the few still moored on the river swans sailed majestically between their hulls. Jon decided he would drive out in the afternoon onto the Isle of Purbeck and visit the village of Corfe with its spectacular castle placed on top of a hill. The ruin was visible for miles and he could remember as a boy visiting the castle tea shop with his Grandmother and feeding himself, fit to burst, with a cream tea and cheese and pickle sandwiches.

He drove over the Frome bridge on to the Isle of Purbeck, not an island but a peninsular sliced from the mainland by the river. The countryside was estuary flat and the marshland was dotted with yellow gorse and purple heather. The sun was just beginning to warm the fields and brighten the land as the road began to climb slightly toward the village of Corfe. In the distance he caught a glimpse of the monolithic towers of the castle ruins.

In the village he parked outside the Greyhound Inn and put on his coat, there was still a cold breeze coming off the coast some five miles away which made the air brisk.

He decided a walk in the castle was what was needed to work up an appetite for tea and scones so he bought a ticket and walked over the old stone bridge up to the castle lawns. He passed a couple of school parties, field trip clip boards in hand, and made his way to a quieter part of the castle.

He found a spot near the old Norman tower, which had threatened to fall down the slope for three centuries. He sat close to it sheltering from the wind and to take in the view over Purbeck and Dorset to the horizon. Sitting, absorbing the atmosphere and glorying in the view, he realised that for the first time in some days he felt at peace.

* * * * *

Corfe Castle

July 1644

Edgar dropped silently down the guttering and peered through the opening that was well camouflaged by trees, bracken and nettles. He could see the shadows of soldiers made by the camp fires that burned in the pitch black of the moonless night. He could hear the bawdy bravado of the Roundheads. He was sure they were boasting of acts of barbarism, rape, torture, pillage and destruction.

He slipped silently through the undergrowth but froze. Only a few feet away a soldier relieved himself in the bushes that blocked his path. Edgar held his breath. After a few minutes the soldier sighed, adjusted his underclothes and returned to his comrades.

Edgar ran across open ground, hoping his sounds would not be heard, towards a sheep track cut along the edge of the camp and stealthily made for the cover of bracken and bramble.

After fighting his way slowly and painfully through the undergrowth for three or four hours, he concealed himself under the fern and slept .

The next morning he was awoken by the sounds of shouts a few hundred yards away from where he had slept. Peering though a gap in the foliage he could make out three young Parliamentarian soldiers dressed in hodden grey collecting firewood and moving in his direction. His heart beat like a thundering drum.

They talked and exchanged jokes. The youngest walked over to where Edgar hid. For one awful moment Edgar thought he'd been spotted.

The boy reached down and picked up a couple of good sized branches and put them into the bundle in his arms. Then, only yards from his hiding place, their arms laden with kindling, they turned back to the camp.

Edgar breathed a sigh of relief rolling over on his back and relaxed, staring at the clear blue sky. He began to notice the morning mist and the chill. He was cold, wet and hungry. He took a few scraps of salt beef from inside his jerkin and gnawed on them ravenously. Crouched in the undergrowth he considered his next move.

He would head to Wareham and cross the River Frome at the heavily guarded bridge. The town was the beginning of the route to Bere Regis and the North, important to the Roundheads.

Hopefully, past this he could make for Blandford Forum over the downs to Shaftsbury and Warminster turning toward Bristol or Oxford depending on the roads and which city was still held by the Royalists.

An hour later he arrived at the bridge in Wareham keeping to the tree line where the ground was quite soft and marshy. He could see each traveller as they were searched, weapons confiscated, women molested, random tolls levied.

Suddenly behind him he heard voices shouting. He had been spotted by a patrol returning to the town and with his heart in his mouth he ran. Behind him the sergeant of the guard had mounted and snatched a sword. Edgar ran for the thicker trees of Wareham forest no more than 100 yards away in an effort to lose them among the dense pine trees and escape. His legs ran for their life and could feel his heart pounding but he kept running.

The horse thundered behind him, so close now he could hear its straining breath. He glanced in panic over his shoulder. Ahead of him he was only a few yards to freedom. The horse and its dark rider were now only a few feet from him. Edgar could smell the horse and it's the rider. He could feel the bulk of the animal and hear the cursing of the rider who whipped the beast forward.

Suddenly he felt a dull thud in his left shoulder as the sword tore into it and another in his back as it pierced his lungs. Edgar collapsed on to the ground in a broken heap. The trees towering over him were becoming dim and with his last desperate and futile movement he crawled toward them.

"So near, the woods. Too young. Not ready. So much to do," and with the sound of song ringing in his head Edgar died.

The soldier pulled the horse up and wheeled it around a few yards ahead. Dismounting he strode over to the body.

The sergeant stood over the corpse of the man he had just murdered. His spirit was black hearted and evil.

"Another soul for my lord !" He thought and smiled in victory.

He took out his flintlock pistol and aimed it at the head.

"Another !" he said pulling the trigger but Edgar had long since departed .

* * * * *

Under the shadow of the ruined Norman tower Jon took in the view over Purbeck and the Dorset to the horizon.

He took a deep breath and closed his eyes momentarily.

And the scene changed...

In his mind's eye he could see himself stealthily crawling through undergrowth. He could the smell the camp fires, the soldiers, their horses, the roasting meat, the nettles and bracken. He had a mission, a message to deliver. It was a pitch black moonless night.

He slipped silently through the undergrowth but froze as only a few feet away a soldier relieved himself in the bushes that blocked his path. He held his breath and then after a few minutes the soldier adjusted his underclothes satisfied and returned to his comrades .

He ran across open ground towards a sheep track cut along the edge and stealthily made for the cover of bracken and bramble.

Then, it was morning. He was cold, wet, hungry. He could smell the damp undergrowth, he could feel the fear.

He must keep to tree line. Ground is marshy and soft. Voices. Shouts. They have seen him.

He ran. Run. Getting closer. Get to trees. Run. Horse. Rider. Sword. Getting closer. Heart pounding. Run. Getting closer.

No ! Pain ! Dark Shadow. Dull Ache. No ! Pain !

Breathless. Falling. Explosion. Singing. Sleeping.

And Jon woke with a start and opened his eyes in the brightness.

In the distance was Brownsea Island and beyond it a ferry sailed toward Poole Harbour.

There was sunlight. There was peace.

He was sweating. He was shaking. He was afraid.

.

* * * * *

"Wake now ! Wake from your slumber ! I need your presence !" The voice was almost reptilian. It hissed and slithered, a voice of evil and possession, "Wake now, Ranulf !"

Ranulf opened his eyes and in the darkness walked to the mirror. His body was tired but his mind was alert. He knew that he could not ignore his master - such a summons was a horrific nightmare from which there was no escape.

"I am your own, master !" Ranulf said staring into the blackness of the mirror.

"Ranulf. Your work for me is appreciated. I have no other who can do such work. You have talent Ranulf, my eternal champion."

There was dark foreboding in the voice, "you must continue your work. The souls you steal give me power in the darkness but wheels are turning. The force of light is moving against us and I will not tolerate their interference."

"What must be done Master ? Can they be defeated ?"

The voice laughed. "Easily ! They are, after, all only mortal. Easily manipulated and easily destroyed..."

"Where must I go ? What should I do ? How can they be found ?"

"Patience Ranulf !" The voice said calmly, "do not be so hungry for action. Soon enough my eternal one. Soon enough"

* * * * *

Jon lay in his bed wondering if sanity was finally leaving him. He had suffered so much in recent years that he had often wished to just leave this earth. He felt fearful of slumber - *to sleep perchance to dream*. He craved a peaceful night but Jon slept and still the voices came...

"Jon do not give up hope, do not be afraid," his brother's voice was pleading but, Jon was silent. "The waking dream you had was of a past life. You saw it because you needed to see it !" Still Jon remained silent, "Jon ! Eric Matheson. You were right. He did not pass through this place, he is one of the lost ones !"

Jon was shocked out of his silence, "you mean he didn't pass over ?"

"He died but didn't pass through the gateway, he is one of the missing."

Jon felt himself drifting back to slumber and the voices faded once again.

* * * * *

There was once a man who lived in a time when magic, black or white, was deemed to be witchcraft. His mother was, to all intents and purposes a doctor, she did not understand her healing powers but her hands were blessed.

As a young man he had almost died from a fever. He had drifted in and out of sleep until he finally felt life's energy coursing through his body. His mother had stayed by his bed through that time, praying to any deity who would listen to help her save her only son.

But in her prayers she had formed a pact with a powerful dark lord that would eventually sacrifice her life and had gifted her son's soul for eternity.

Twelve months to the day after his recovery his mother was burnt at the stake by a priest for practising witchcraft.

From that moment onward he knew that the only power of worth was that of evil. He would worship only darkness and he would destroy and this would be his creed - to kill for his master of darkness !

Since that time he had fought in many battles and had met and killed many men, good and evil, he cared not.

He had terminated the lives of the weak so that his strength could prevail and live on. Over the centuries he had seen all things. Nothing had shaken him from this course.

He had been in the bunker moments before it had been taken, been by the side of Presidents moments before the gunman struck, eaten at tables knowing he was suspected of treachery.

Over the years he had become an eternal champion of this cause. Strong. Invincible. Powerful. He honoured his Lord.

As for love ? It was a word that was now alien to him. In his time he had loved only once. But never again. Never.

Annelise had copied the pages from the prayer book onto music manuscript using the limited musical knowledge with which she was gifted and passed them to Doktor Koenig, a professor of music at the University of Stuttgart who now sat with her studying the piece.

The Doktor scanned the sheets and placed them on top of the piano. He took a deep breath and played. The piece was glorious, sublime, honey, nectar for the soul. It was one of the most beautiful pieces they had ever heard instantly etching onto their souls. The music ended with a crescendo of sound that she could imagine played with choir and orchestra. The last chord resonated around the room making every object in it vibrate with the music of bass notes.

Doktor Koenig lifted his hands gently from the keyboard and took a deep breath. He seemed emotionally drained. After arranging his thoughts he spoke. "Where did you get this ? It is wonderful ! Where did you find it ?" The doctor asked intensely.

"It was a gift ! Do you have any idea who composed it ?" Annelise asked in reply.

The doctor laughed. "You are joking my dear. You really have no idea ?" He laughed again. "It's undoubtedly Wolfgang Amadeus Mozart. It was written late in his life but it is Mozart. His melodic signatures are incontrovertible. There are minor mistakes of course but I would imagine they are transposition errors made by yourself. Mozart's handwriting was never the best, he would never have made such mistakes himself."

Annelise smiled. "Have you any idea when it was written ?"

Koenig ran his fingers through his hair and thought for a moment. "Well my dear," he said "I may be wrong but I believe it was written around 1787 or 1788. It is possibly the fabled piece missing from his Requiem."

"The Requiem ? Is that possible ?" Annelise was wide eyed.

Koenig nodded, "Let me explain. It was rumoured that in 1787 Mozart wrote the last movement to his Requiem, a Glorianna. We have this from documentary evidence written by a priest in Prague where Mozart had just produced the opera Don Giovanni. After Mozart's death the Requiem was completed by Mozart's pupil based on a few scribblings and the scholar's own ideas. Mozart knew the last passage should be glorious and majestic, that it should be his epitaph - dedicated to the magnificence of God ! Sadly, Mozart died before his time and we thought this piece died with him. From what I can see here, Annelise, Mozart did indeed compose his Glorianna."

Chapter 9

Earth Bound Misfit

"No man can ever know the consequences of his actions. In this way blame can be reallocated to the blameless. But, every action has an equal an opposite inaction and for evil to triumph it is only necessary for good men to do nothing."

Jarrat Toldon, Chronicles of the Future

"Into the distance a ribbon of black, stretched to the point of no turning back."

David Gilmour

*T*hat night Jon dreamt of his favourite of cities. A city of spires and copper domes and castles. Salzburg was a city of many characters and Jon and his wife had enjoyed every one of them. They had last visited Salzburg twelve months ago for Christmas and it was one of the most romantic times they had spent.

Jon woke with a fresh sense of purpose. He felt armed with spiritual strength and direction. The voices had told him southward and in the absence of any firmer information Salzburg was the direction he would take. Somehow his intuition told him that this was correct.

He showered, shaved and dressed and took breakfast overlooking the garden. He could hear the wood pigeons coo on the roof as they were warmed by the early morning sunshine. After a walk in the garden he went back to his room and phoned the airline. He managed to reserve a seat on an early evening flight with Air Austria that would get him to a hotel by ten.

With a morning to waste he walked around the town of Wareham that was beginning to bustle with market day shoppers. He visited the tiny museum with its memorabilia of Lawrence of Arabia who had died in a motor cycle accident nearby. He walked along the river to Redcliffe feeding the ducks and swans around the bridge and took tea in Nellie Crumb's.

After a light lunch he began his journey to Heathrow. The traffic built up as he approached the outskirts of the sprawling metropolis. With plenty of time to spare he arrived at the airport and checked in over an hour before his flight. He had left his car in the long stay car park, guessing he would only be away only a few days. Sadly in this his intuition was wrong.

* * * * *

Heathrow Airport

June 2071

The plans for the new underground car park had been passed by the Southern England Greater Metropolitan Council to aid the heavy congestion around the airport that coped with hundreds of thousands of passengers every day.

In line with stringent conservation laws the archaeologists had surveyed the building, drawn it and photographed it and were satisfied that the late 1960's example of concrete architecture had been documented. After a storm of protests that had been (and were always going to be) unsuccessful the building could now be demolished.

Before this could begin all floors were to be cleared of debris. The car park had been closed for over a month and most of the dozen floors were empty. A few abandoned and probably stolen vehicles had been towed away for claim or resale.

On the 11th floor was one last vehicle. Its tyres were almost rotten and it had years of thick dust on its silver paint work. Removing the grime from the windscreen and number plates the attendant had tried to work out the age of the vehicle but had been unable to recognise the yellow back plate seven character serial number.

The next day it was loaded onto a transporter and sent to the English Motor Museum of Beaulieu in Hampshire. There it was cleaned, carefully restored and almost a year later shown to the public.

The car was an Opel Monza GSE 3.0 Litre that showed over 200,000 miles on it's milometer. It shone like the day it was new.

It had been built in Rudeshiem in what was Germany in February 1986. The paint work and engine were in perfect condition. It was the only surviving example of this type of petrol driven vehicle left in the United States of Europe and was worth many million Euro.

Researchers had said it was incredible that it had survived in such good condition all those years.

It had never been broken into, damaged or tampered with. In such a car park it was almost incredible that should be the case. It was as if it had a guardian angel watching over it.

Historians, archivists and researchers had been unable to trace the owner.

* * * * *

Back in his apartment Drew had, through visits to the library, managed to gather more information about the chess piece. Jeremiah Monday had also discover that it was possibly the missing king from a set now shown in the Scottish Museum of Antiquities in Edinburgh. The museum had sent him the history of the set that seemed to indicate it was buried on the Isle of Lewis in the Hebrides at about 1500 and was made in Scandinavia around the 12th century.

The question therefore was how could a 12th century chess piece get separated from its brothers and find it's way across the Atlantic and nearly 3000 miles of the American continent to Yosemite ? Even if he could answer this question he still didn't understand its significance.

Exhausted with these thoughts Drew slept soundly and dreamed of a city he had never visited. A city of spires and copper domes and castles. It was a baroque city of many characters. He dreamt of Salzburg.

* * * * *

Ranulf had watched many battles and was unmoved by the destruction and waste of life. He was waiting for the moment when he was ordered to move, when he felt the rush of energy that filled him with life. Once he had wished he could escape hating the visions, to be free of these nightmares but he had come to enjoy the darkness.

He was a warrior. He had killed many men and he had been *killed* by many men. He could display the scars of numerous fights, skirmishes and battles. He had been dust many times. He did not fear death, indeed he had embraced it like a friend many times. He had been reborn and resurrected many times.

For all that, for so much sorrow as joy and for so much laughter as pain, still the net result was zero.

He knew that if all the generals and admirals and politicians could see the death he had witnessed there would never be another war. The concept of mankind destroying mankind was bizarre. To be killed in the name of peace loving Gods, a line on a map, the colour of one's skin or a tattered cloth in the breeze was utter stupidity yet still it continued.

Ranulf had realised that if Jesus came again to walk amongst the faithless, if he stood in the town squares and taught new lessons no one would want to listen to him trapped in their selfish world. Ranulf was trapped in his own hell eternal, where purgatory was every waking moment and rest was a dreamless sleep and Ranulf, the soul less man, had never realised that he lived at the bottom of a deep abyss and that hell was on earth.

* * * * *

Yugoslavia

Winter 1994

The shots he wanted were on the other side of the meadow where the machine gun fire originated. If he kept low and dragged the camera along the ground he would be safe. They would be the shots the syndicates would pay the earth for. Behind the shelter of the building his reporter remained safe, watching for snipers.

Gingerly the cameraman approached the hedge and crouched low. He held the camera to his eye and filmed. There they were, shooting toward the barn.

Suddenly he heard the sound of a ricochet and felt a searing pain in his shoulder. The last thing he saw was the shattering of glass as the second sniper's bullet pierced the lens and drilled into his brain.

Ranulf watched impassively, patiently and unseen as the corpse of the cameraman fell to the earth and the camera and its video were dashed on the floor. Ranulf's moment in the drama had arrived.

Ranulf remembered the first voices like a nightmare, haunting and vivid. He could not escape from them. He had realised that he needed a fix and now as much as they relied on him, he relied on them. He had become addicted to its rush and now they were somehow comforting. Then the spell came to him, the chant that would take him to the wait state. He uttered the first syllables and felt the rush of movement downwards travelling on a descending lift. Then with a sudden jolt he was moving upwards and with a blinding flash of white and he was at the false gateway.

"Come now my lost one ! Come now !" His voice was soft, calm and soothing.

The soul drifted upwards leaving body, broken camera and final searing pain on the earth. It floated high above the scene until it was just a speck. Then, it heard a voice, a soothing voice, a voice of welcome, a singing voice.

"Come now my lost one ! Come now !" Ranulf said softly.

The soul felt so weak and tired, drifting onward and upward. Then it saw the white door and it gently reached out to touch it. The soul moved toward it and could see a shadow greeting it beside the door.

"Come this way my lost one ! Come this way !" Ranulf said softly.

The door opened and the soul stepped through it.

Into darkness. Into eternity. Into the abyss.

The New World

October 1492

For eight weeks the Pinta, Nina and Santa Maria had sailed on into the unknown. They had sailed into the sunset hoping to find a direct Western passage to the riches of the Indies. Columbus knew if he sailed a few degrees northward he would hit the southern tip of the old Viking land of Vinland. If he kept to his course he would sail to the South of the island and onto the coast of China.

A few days before the crew had become restless, threatening mutiny but, the sighting of a seagull had put pay to that. Columbus was beginning to regret his choice of sailing westward rather than sailing down the coast of Vinland and then to the West. It was a gamble he hoped would still pay off. He was convinced it was there.

Early in the morning of October 12th 1492 the lookout spotted vegetation through the cold mists. The crew caught glimpses of trees, a beach, a hill. They heard strange bird calls and could feel the warmth of the land.

They dropped anchor and waited for the mist to clear. They were moored in a wide bay of a large island that they did not recognise, it looked so unfamiliar to them. Columbus ordered a boat to be launched and a landing party to be formed. He and ten heavily armed men took to the boat and rowed ashore. Standing at the prow of the boat he could see the sea breaking on an alien shore. The boat beached itself on the sand and Columbus waded through the shallow breakers washing on the warm white sand until his boots made footprints on a new world. Columbus fell to his knees in prayer and exhaustion. A flag was planted and the kingdom was claimed for their majesties Ferdinand and Isabella of Spain.

Columbus had discovered the islands of what is now Haiti. The islands of the West Indies were inhospitable and the gold for which the Spanish crown sought was never found. Columbus never found the western passage and died close to poverty and anonymity. The continent which blocked Columbus' path was discovered by Amerigo Vespucio and was named America after him.

The quest for riches and wealth that drove expeditions wiped out families, cities and civilisations. It is a greed that still lives on 500 years later.

To some Columbus was a failure, to some he was a madman and to others he was a visionary. But, if Columbus achieved anything it was that one's dreams can last longer than the night.

* * * * *

Back in her apartment Annelise was trying to understand what she could do. To have found such a valuable piece of music was beyond comprehension. Mozart had died in suspicious circumstances, at least that was what the conspiracy theories seemed to say, but she did not understand the significance of Reinhardt's gift.

The question that buzzed in her head was how could an 18th century prayer book containing one of the greatest pieces of music ever written find its way into Reinhardt's hands in 1943. Even if she could answer this question she still didn't quite understand its significance.

Her head spun with the problem and she felt exhausted. She took a hot bath and went to her bed with a glass of Ansbacher Brandy and slept soundly.

That night she dreamed of a city she had never visited. A city of spires and copper domes and castles. It was a city of many characters. It was Mozart's city, it was the city of Salzburg.

*****

The plane was quiet and Jon had been given a window seat just in front of the wing with plenty of leg room. He enjoyed flying and the buzz of escaping the irresistible force of gravity. The stewardess explained the safety instructions while the club class passengers were already becoming restless, impatient for their G & T's and smoked salmon.

The 737 sped along the tarmac as the light faded and the first glow of sunset began to paint the skies. A roar of engines and Jon felt pushed back in his seat as it passed effortlessly through the air leaving a vortex of vapour trails in its wake.

The sky was cloudless and in the gathering dusk beads of orange marked the subdivisions of suburbia with pinpoints of light. Clusters of light mapped out a village or town, pin pricks marked a farm house, a cottage, a pub. Motorways slithered across the pitch black land with the occasional clover leaf intersection.

The earth was far below him and the world slipped into slumber. All but one of its number.

Jon looked at the miniature landscape laid out below him and prayed that there was a soul who wouldn't be beaten by the creeping arthritis of indecision, ineptitude and insignificance. There had to be someone in that sea of dim light who held the keys to what was a holistic problem.

Fortunately, Jon's prayers were about to be answered.

Chapter 10.

Crossing Paths

"There were times when men were unaware of their destinies. They felt fear and apprehension as the road ahead was unclear. It was at times such as these that men who could not find a way struck out and made new roads themselves."

Jarrat Toldon, Chronicles of the Future

*"On the outskirts of nowhere, on the ring road to somewhere,
On the verge of indecision, I'll always take the round about way."*

Derek W Dick

The pilot eased the plane through the mountains and landed on the short runway of Salzburg airport. It was a brisk cold moonlit night and the airport was quiet. Jon picked up his bag from the conveyer and took a taxi to the Hotel Schloss Moenstein an old castle hotel set on a hill above the city and away from the traffic and tourist bustle.

The hotel was luxurious and Jon had a few guilt pangs about his credit card taking a pounding. He asked for a single room but the hotel was quiet and instead they gave him the larger Tower Room with windows on four sides and spectacular views of the castle and city.

He rang room service to order sandwiches and a glass of wine and settled in for the evening. It was already 10:30 and it had been a long day.

He lay on the bed in the dark, curtains open, looking out at the moon and stars. The sky reflected the bright lights that illuminated the magnificent city buildings. In the distance he could hear the hum of the city.

He closed the curtains, pulled back the blankets and slipped between the crisp white starched sheets. He closed his eyes and wished his wife was there, smiling to himself as he thought of her. He reviewed his journey so far and wondered what tomorrow held. What was he to do ? He didn't know why he was in this city but he was convinced he was supposed to be here.

With the distant hum of traffic in his head he drifted into a deep sleep.

* * * * *

73

Early next morning Drew's aircraft touched down on Austrian soil. He felt tired and jet lagged and the stopover in Vienna had been a nightmare. All he wanted was to shower and sleep. He picked up his luggage and went to the information desk for advice on hotels.

"Hi ! I'm in town for a few days and I need a hotel not too far from the action and not too pricey." he said.

The girl looked up from her PC screen and beamed at the man at her counter. Luckily, she spoke English but always felt annoyed when Americans assumed all foreigners could.

"Well sir," she said handing him a leaflet, "I recommend the Hotel Schaffenrath. It's on a main bus route and it's not too expensive. A little over a mile from the town centre."

"Sounds great !" Drew seeing his goal now in site, "where can I get a taxi ?" The girl pointed out the front doors and taxi rank beyond.

Ten minutes later Drew was checking into the Schaffenrath. It looked a cosy hotel and the staff were friendly. The receptionist, dressed in a traditional Austrian dirndl, showed him to his room. He decided he would get a drink from the bar, then shower and to bed.

At the bar, the receptionist walked across from the check-in desk to the bar and served him. "Zu trinken sir ?" She asked.

He wasn't quite switched onto German and thought there might be something wrong. He'd managed to grab a word which sounded like drink ,"Oh yeah, do you have tea ?"

"Tea sir ? With milch ?" The conversation was difficult but progressed.

"Oh yes. Milk. Sure." Drew replied. He knew he should have listened in those high school German classes.

Moments later and the girl returned carrying a tray with a large blue willow pattern cup with a tea bag draped over the side, a jug of hot milk, a few sachets of sugar and a large biscuit. She placed it in front of Drew and returned to the check in desk.

He made up the brew, sweet and milky. As he dunked the biscuit in the liquid he felt the pressures of the last 24 hours begin to wash from his body. He felt very relaxed and tired. Some minutes later, teacup drained, Drew was slumped at the counter, snoozing peacefully.

* * * * *

Annelise had found the drive south from Stuttgart an easy one, except for the abysmal traffic system around Munich and the suicidal BMW and Mercedes drivers on the autobahn. The customs guard had given only a cursory glance at her passport and she was driving on the yellow dashed roads of Austria.

If she remembered correctly in her teens she used to stay with her parents in a hotel about four kilometres from Salzburg close to the Untersberg mountain. She pulled off the autobahn and took the route southwards. Within minutes, her memory serving her well, she pulled up on the hotel car park. The hotel was a traditional family run hotel built in a Tyrollian chalet style just as she had remembered, it was right under the Untersberg mountain and the cable car to the summit left right next door.

She checked into the hotel and was shown to cosy pine panelled room with a view of the mountain and the cable car. She threw back the windows and took a deep breath of clear fresh mountain air, the chill of the late afternoon was beginning to come down. After a shower she sat on the bed reading a book, having picked up a biography the day before about Mozart and his last years.

There were a number of conspiracies involving his death. Some favoured the Illuminati, an elite clique of masons who had allegedly financed an assassination due to secrets revealed in the Magic Flute. Other theories discussed the strained relationship with court composer Salieri and the possibility of his jealousy toward Mozart and his talent.

Mozart's health deteriorated quickly in the last few months of his life. If it wasn't due to kidney failure as some doctors had hypothesised, but was due to poison then someone must have had daily access to Mozart over those months.

Annelise favoured the theory concerning the husband of one of Mozart's many lovers. The day after Mozart's death one of his pupils, a young married woman in her late twenties whom he saw regularly, was viciously stabbed by her husband. The husband subsequently hung himself from the rafters of his living room and the woman who manage to survived was committed to a mental asylum.

Annelise mulled over the theories as she got ready for bed. She rolled down the shutters and turned off the light. In the bar below her she could hear laughter and singing but it didn't seem to disturb her, indeed it was quite comforting.

She mentally planned her next day with a visit to the Mozarteum and Mozart's birthplace and definitely a walk along Getriedegasse. With the thoughts of the city and music in her head she drifted off to sleep.

* * * * *

Toledo, Spain

1490

Count Orgaz felt that today was a good day to die. If he fell he would do so fighting the usurpers to rid Castilla of the Moor, win back Toledo for his Queen and unfurl the banner of Santa Iago over the Alcazar. God would be on the side of the victors today !

His small chosen band of worthies followed him unquestioningly. They fought like warriors and in their wake men fell like rag dolls onto the cobbled alleyways. He wealded his father's Toledo Salamanca, a long blade, balanced and razor sharp but dulled now with the blood of the dead it had dispatched in the battle.

Around him the screams of the dying and yelps of the those surprised by death, the battle raged. They were close now to their goal, close to the gates of the cathedral where the final push would come. His men would have the honour of being the first into that tainted and desecrated place !

Behind him down a side alley two of his men, Jose, a bear of a man and Carlos, a young pup who had joined for the glory, had been cornered by five of the Turks wealding scimitars and screaming with bloodlust. Without hesitation Don Orgaz turned to help his men. He immediately dispatched the first before the Arab realised death was at his shoulder.

As he parried and thrust into flesh he felt renewed strength. Could it be possible he was enjoying the barbaric task before him.

Turning to face the last of the five that still stood he saw a sudden look of horror in Jose's eyes, as if he had seen a ghost. At that moment he felt a dull ache in his back that welled into a searing pain in his stomach. He looked down to see the point of a spear dripping with his life's blood.

The blade fell from his trembling hand and Jose immediately killed the assassin and caught his master's falling body in one fluid movement. Don Orgaz slumped on the ground with the battle and the shouts of his men blurring into a hazy dreamscape.

He remembered his wife, his son and then as if in a dream his father and mother, childhood days, the smell of incense and summer sunshine on his back. All these things he saw through dimming eyes and unconsciously he reached from the blade and his finger tip touched the bloody golden pommel.

"Too soon," he sighed and with songs of angels in his ears he left this earth.

* * * * *

Vienna

7th December 1791

A pauper's burial was a very regular occurrence and the gravediggers saw nothing special about this one, especially when there was nothing to be made from the deceased's chattels.

The body had been stripped of anything of value and placed into old stitched flour sacks. The top had been tied with an unusual golden cord, a gift from a local dignitary. The clothes the corpse wore had suggested perhaps a more dignified burial but orders had been given for it to be in the pauper's communal grave.

Grod and Polny, the gravediggers, placed the body in a temporary coffin, a box strong enough to carry the body and tip it into the pit at the grave side. Once they had despatched the body and shovelled lime onto it to keep down the stench, their job would be done and their pay earnt.

As the cart clattered along the mud road the snow started to fall and an eerie silence surrounded them. They wrapped themselves up as best as they could against the bitter cold and pulled the horse up at the pit. They pulled up rags over their mouths to lessen the stench in their nostrils and Grod slid back the coffin lid. He pulled back the top of the sack and went through a final search for valuables. Grod cursed, there were no gold teeth, no silver buttons, no wig, nothing from which he could make a few coppers.

He checked the commodious pockets. Sometimes the odd coin or pin would have been overlooked. He felt something heavy in an inside pocket, a wallet perhaps ? No, not a wallet and he grunted as he took from the pocket a small black prayer book.

He thought for a moment and felt sure old Hirschfelden in the town would pay a good price for it. Hirschfelden liked books and might pay a few crowns for this one. He dropped it into his long-coat pocket and retied the sacking over the corpse replacing the coffin lid then, quite unceremoniously they bundled the coffin from the cart and over to the side of the pit.

The ground was muddy and slippery with the fresh snow and they were careful not to go too close to the edge. Polny looked at Grod who nodded and they tipped up the coffin . The flap opened and the body dropped into the pit feet first. They crossed themselves as some small mark of respect, after all they would both be laid to rest in one pit or another sometime in the hopefully distant future.

Polny shovelled a measure of lime onto the rotting corpses, threw the shovel aside and hopped back onto the cart where Grod was already examining the book.

"Halves ?" said Grod. Polny shrugged in tacit agreement.

The next day Grod arrived early at the booksellers. He slid the book over the counter and the bookseller pulled on his spectacles.

"How much ?" he asked.

Hirschfelden examined the book, occasionally tutting and shaking his head. It was an ordinary prayer book, a little worn and somewhat jaded but Hirschfelden thought he would offer the man one guilder. The gravedigger would be happy with a nights drinking money.

"A guilder !" Grod said in disgust, "I can sell it for two to a pious man !"

Hirschfelden took out the money, "Find one !" He said giving the book back to the gravedigger.

Grod looked at it wondering whether to bargain. He decided against it and nodded in acceptance.

Hirschfelden handed him the coin, "Much obliged to you sir" and with that Grod bowed and scurried from the shop, in case questions might be asked of its source. Grod was very happy with the profit he had made.

As soon as the shop door closed, Hirschfelden ran over and locked it. Excitedly, he picked up the book from the counter, opening it to the back cover. He felt sure he had seen something remarkable during his hurried examination.

There written on the back pages was music. Scored, lined and perfectly orchestrated. Music of such glory and magnificence. Music for the angels to sing.

He recognised the style immediately for he had seen its composer perform many times at various parties and functions to which he had been invited. He had even become an artistic admirer of the man. He flicked to the back cover to confirm his suspicions and there written in black ink was the date and the autograph for which he sought:

W. A. Prague 1787

Chapter 11

"Close...But Not Touching"

"They tried to cheat it, imploring their masters to allow them to stay, making one squalid bargain after another. They did not know that such bargains perpetuated the hells in which they lived"

Jarrat Toldon, Chronicles of the Future

"A momentary lapse of reason, which binds a life to a life"

David Gilmour

*J*on awoke refreshed after a good nights sleep with his rest unbroken by the voices that had been troubling him lately.

He pulled back the curtains and gazed across the city of Salzburg dominated by the impressive castle that had stood guard for six centuries over the area. The copper roofs gleamed in the early morning sun and the air was crisp and clear. He took a deep breath and felt ready for action.

He ate a hearty breakfast in the restaurant, exchanged pleasantries with the receptionist and walked briskly toward the lift that would take him down to street level.

Ten minutes later he was looking down along the narrow Getriedegasse with its wrought iron signs that gave it a distinctly mediaeval flavour. The street was already bustling with early morning shoppers and a few tourists making the most of the day. It was blocked with vans bringing the day's deliveries to the shops and restaurants and the scene was a little chaotic. He bought a newspaper and walked to the Residenz Square where he sat on a bench and watched the tourists gathering around the horse drawn carriages discussing fares with the drivers dressed in long green coats and alpine hats.

In the distance, close to the Glockenspiel tower he could see the over ornate statue of Mozart, its base adorned with flowers from an admirer.

He opened the Salzburger Nachrichten and scanned the news, most of which would be of more interest to the locals. He found himself scrutinising the entertainment pages.

A concert of chamber music was scheduled for that evening in the Residenz outside which he was sitting. He decided to ask the receptionist to get hold of a ticket for him when he returned to the hotel. If anyone contacted him he would have to put them off.

He folded his newspaper and took a walking tour of the city. The main part of the city was familiar to him but he suspected there were still discoveries to be made across the river.

He walked back along Getriedegasse, crossed the busy thoroughfare that ringed the city and then the bridge that led to Linzegasse. The street was as narrow as Getriedegasse but less ornate, the shops more day to day concerned with food, footwear and fashion. His window shopping brought him to an antique shop, its window crammed with interesting artefacts. He was always on the look out for an old chess set and decided to take a look inside.

Opening the door set a string of bells jingling. An old man carefully put down the delicate musical box he was reassembling and peered over his spectacles to survey Jon. "Gruss Gott, mein Herr. Kann ich Ihnen hilfen ?" He asked.

"Nein danke." Jon began to scramble for his lost German vocabulary, "I am sorry but, do you speak English ?"

"But, of course !" Came the reply and Jon heaved a small sigh of relief.

"Do you mind if I take a look around. I'm not really looking for anything in particular."

"Certainly !" The proprietor said smiling and nodding ryely, "take your time !"

Jon felt he didn't know where to start. He could see all manner of items that caught his eye, a watch, an old clock, a pack of cards, a pewter jug. Eventually he came to a tall glass cabinet with a row of 19th century Napoleonic swords displayed in it.

"I can see you like beautiful blades " the owner's voice came from behind him startling Jon as he was so engrossed in the contents of the display case, "but, one moment, I have something that may interest you, one moment please !"

The old man scurried excitedly to the back room and returned with what appeared to be a hessian sack. He placed it on the counter and peeled back the wrapping revealing an oily greaseproof paper package.

Jon caught a glimpse of gold and steel and then, his heart beating faster, it was revealed to be old Spanish sword.

"Beautiful is it not ?" The old man said. "It is a Toledo Salamanca. Made around 1485. It is a work of art !"

The hilt was studded with sapphires, opals and rubies. Jon extended his hand to feel the gold wire wrapped around the pommel. It was certainly a magnificent weapon. The old man picked it up and offered it to Jon who took it without hesitation. He grasped the hilt and drew the sword from its scabbard.

The sword fitted his hand exactly and he felt the perfect balance of it. The sword could have been made for him, indeed it seemed to feel as if it was an old friend. He held the steel to the light to look closely at the slight curve on the blade and noticed the scrollwork at the base of the blade which simply said :

$$\mathcal{D}on \; O_{rgaz} \; 1485$$

The sword gleamed in the sunlight as if cast and beaten only yesterday.

For a moment he felt slightly nauseous and the world seemed to stand still. A warm, dull pain began in his back and welled in his stomach. Knocking the scabbard to the floor he managed to place the sword on the counter before doubling up in agony, dropping to his knees and clutching his stomach. He could hear the sound of battle in his ears, feel the pain of a fatal wound and he remembered the remorse of death. Then, he blacked out.

He came round a few minutes later with the pain subsiding. The old man was kneeling next to him shaking his head.

"It is a painful reminder is it not ?" The old man said.

"What do you mean ?" Jon asked perhaps already guessing the answer.

"One of your many pasts has returned to remind you. It is quite simple," and the old man helped Jon to a chair. "I ought to introduce myself. My name is Hirschfelden. My family has minded this sword for many years" He slid the blade back into its scabbard. "We were given it in payment of services rendered on the condition that we pass it on at the right time. I shall be sad to see it go." And he stroked the scabbard like a beloved pet.

Jon felt a little better, though dazed, not only by the experience but by what he was being told. "Can I purchase it ?" Jon asked.

Hirschfelden laughed, "Such a sword is priceless ! It is one of a kind ! It is made for one purpose and only you will know what that purpose shall be."

With that he began to rewrap the sword in its sacking, certainly poor cloth for such a treasure. He then placed the bundle in a long cardboard flower box and sealed the lid with tape.

"Now you must go. Take the sword with my and my ancestor's blessing. Use it well and may God be with you !" Hirschfelden passed the package to Jon who tucked it under his arm.

"Thank you !" Jon said.

"You're very welcome. Remember. For evil to triumph..."

But, Jon finished the proverb for him, "it is only enough for good men to do nothing ?"

"Quite so," there was a slight sadness in the man's eyes, "Please. Enjoy your stay in Salzburg."

Hirschfelden warmly shook Jon's hand and smiled at him giving Jon the impression that the man knew more about Jon's future than he did.

Jon walked back out into Linzergasse in a dream. He felt exhausted by his ordeal and hoped his Hotel would revive him as it had done so often before.

On his return to the hotel an envelope on his bedside table awaited his attention. It was addressed to him and written on the back was :

Enjoy the Concert.

Afterwards, the Schloss Gastezimmer

Zetter

In the envelope was a front row ticket for the evening's Residenz concert. Jon smiled and shook his head. The picture was beginning to form.

He leaned back and his head touched the down filled pillow. He slept until six.

* * * * *

Drew had decided to take a city tour. It seemed the best way to get to know the sights and would be easier on the feet. By lunch time he'd seen all he wanted to see and had taken a table on Cafe Tomaseli's balcony where he had picked up a newspaper, ordered a pot of hot coffee and relaxed watching the activity in the square.

Salzburg was busy with tourists being herded from one sight to another *doing* the Mozart tour. Across the square he watched a group of Japanese tourists who followed a woman in traditional Austrian dress and waving what looked like a car aerial with a pink lace handkerchief tied to it. On the other side of the square another group had gathered at the base of the Glockenspiel that played something which Drew thought resembled a piece of Mozart or Beethoven, he wasn't sure. It was classical anyway.

He had also noticed a young woman window shopping in the more expensive boutiques in the square. She was quite attractive and Drew decided from her dress she was probably German or Austrian. Suddenly she turned her head seemingly aware someone was staring at her. Drew lowered his gaze to his newspaper out of embarrassment and the woman smiled as she walked across the square towards the Glockenspiel. Drew watched over the top of the newspaper as she crossed the square.

Annelise had been to Salzburg many times before. She had spent the mid morning sitting on the Hohensalzburg terrace with a glass of wine and a good book basking in the hazy sunshine. She loved Salzburg's narrow streets and adored the shops that had a superb selection of French, Italian and German fashions.

In Salzburg especially, it was not unusual for her to be stared at, she was attractive and made the most of her figure, but she had felt the man at the cafe almost burning holes in the back of her head. She sighed and decided it was time for a late lunch back at the hotel.

On the other side of the square Drew had made the same decision and resolved to take a taxi back to the Schaffenrath.

At their respective hotels they were each handed an envelope containing a ticket for a concert at the Residenz Palace. The envelope was correctly addressed with few clues as to the identity of the sender, just a simple message :

Enjoy the Concert.

Afterwards, the Schloss Gastezimmer

Zelter

* * * * *

The old man sat back in his comfortable old leather chair. A fire blazed in the small hearth though it was relatively warm outside.

Salzburg had always seemed a cold and damp city to him and he preferred the warmer climate of Vienna. However he had had no choice in the venue for the meeting.

"Well," he thought toasting himself with port, "they have arrived. I did not think they would, but they have come !"

In his head a voice angelic and patient said, "well done. Well done. You've done well. Yet again, you have attained your goal !" The voice congratulated him.

It was a voice that Zetler recognised as that of his guardian. It had aided and comforted him for many years. It was a voice of love and calm. It was neither masculine nor feminine but it was a loving voice.

One day soon he knew they would meet but until that time he had a task to complete and until that time he would fight with purpose and energy to achieve it.

He had thought at one time it was his obsession and perhaps that was true. He regarded it as his quest. He knew many relied on him and he knew many would not rest until what must be done was done.

He had realised long since that his purpose was a simple one.

To right a wrong.

To seek the truth and shout it from the highest mountain top.

To follow the right path until he reached his goal.

He thought of his mother, who had walked the earth many times. What was it she used to say to him as a boy ? "Nothing is ever lost son ! You have just not looked in the right place !" She was right.

In the pitch black of evil, truth was not only hard to find but was so very poorly lit.

It was time to light the first of many candles.

* * * * *

Ranulf sat in the smoky bar listening to the bawdy conversations of the customers. He watched them as a hunter views his quarry ever ready for a kill.

He drew slowly on his cigarette savouring its perfume and tasting the nicotine. He sipped at a crusted dirty glass of vodka.

During the evening, the hookers, thinking he might be the only customer with money, had tried to proposition him. He had turned down their offers. The kick from his vice was economical and beyond sexual satisfaction.

He thought of his present purpose.

Tomorrow he would leave the carnage of Sarajevo and journey to Salzburg a mere five hours drive away. He would miss Sarajevo, it was a city with plenty of potential for him but duty called.

He drew on the cheap cigarette and blew a halo of smoke that rose into the battered shade of the dim light that illuminated the corner of the bar.

"So," he thought to himself, "there are four of them against my one. They have no idea what a dangerous and futile game they are getting themselves in to. And one of their number is a woman too. They send a woman to destroy me ?" He tutted at their apparent naiveity.

As he stood up he downed the final dregs of the vodka and finished the cigarette.

Buttoning his long leather coat he mused, "Now that their pitiful and predictable opening moves have been made we move toward the end game. They will come to learn how powerful a single man can become."

He dropped the smouldering cigarette butt onto the floor and screwed it into the boards with his foot until is was a dirty smear on the floor.

He walked purposefully to the door. There was work to be done !

* * * * *

Berlin

May 6th 1945

His sight was failing. He felt old and tired.

He and his people had achieved so much but ultimately their lack of drive had failed him. The end had come so quickly. If only they had had his vision.

He nodded to the young officer who saluted him and closed the door. He heard the key turn in the door.

He turned to his new bride and he embraced her. She felt so warm, so young, so tender and so close. He remembered happier days in the mountains of Bavaria.

"So my love another journey begins..." he said taking her small hand and they sat on the couch toasting themselves in sparkling German wine.

She drained the glass, put it on the coffee table and held his hand. She picked up the vial and smiled at her husband, kissing him softly and tenderly on the cheek.

"Liebling, mein Liebling !" She said. He closed his eyes and he heard the crack of broken glass. She fell inert to the ground knocking over the vase of summer flowers he had given her.

He picked up the vial in his left hand, putting it to his lips and holding it between his teeth. He held the pistol in his right hand and placed it gently at his temple. He took a final glance of remorse at his wife, lover and mistress lying before him on the plush blue carpet. With a last deep breath and a resigned sigh he bit into the capsule and simultaneously pulled the trigger.

Outside the room they heard the shot.

The Fuhrer and his wife were dead.

But, in that final second, one that had lasted a lifetime, he felt sure, through his tears that he had seen a dark shadow smiling as him, waiting to guide him to a better world.

Ranulf smiled. He was indeed following close behind.

Chapter 12

Visionary

"As a soul is carried from one earthly body to another, in moving from one vessel to another it learns feelings, weaknesses and strengths. And as it learns it's aim is to progress upward on the spiritual ladder until it has gathered all it needs to be a spirit of Elysium. Sadly, there are also those who do not know this. But, once they do, they may make the first steps to Nirvana !"

Jarrat Toldon - Chronicles of the Future

"Don't you know what means the earth to one or few
Can mean just nothing, nothing, nothing to another"

Genesis

*J*on began the evening at the Cafe Winkler where he could watch the daylight fade and the city light up with a substantial meal that included the specialities of Salzburger Nockerl, roast venison and cream of potato soup.

After spending a moment on the terrace surveying the roofscape below he took the lift down into the city and walked along Getriedegasse to Residenzplatz. In the palace he was shown to his seat for the concert.

That evening the music of Bach, Haydn and Mozart echoed through the ornate rooms and corridors of the Residenz, out of the open windows and into the streets and the squares of Salzburg. Jon believed he was part of a perpetual tapestry stitched through years, each note added a fleck of colour and a point of bright light. He soaked up the harmonies and drank in the sound as it washed into his soul.

During the 17th century Mozart had played his first compositions as the boy genius in the same room. His music was synthesised into the walls and into the gold ceilings of the baroque palace.

At the interval, Jon sipped champagne and nibbled Mozart kugeln, balls of chocolate praline, while watching the concert goers with interest.

In the second half the quintet of the Mozarteum played Eine Kleine Nachtmusik, somehow appropriate to the occasion. A rapturous applause signified the concert was over.

Jon picked up his programme as a souvenir and asked one of the ushers to direct him to the Gastsalon, a small room off the main hall. He walked in and settled into a seat next to the elaborate tiled heater.

The usher then walked over and spoke to a young man who was in another corner of the room studying one of the impressive portraits that adorned the walls. A young woman, probably German judging from her outfit and manner, sat sipping wine and he acknowledged her with a nod.

The room had a silence of expectancy that was finally broken when the door opened and an older man was ushered in.

"Good evening everyone, I do hope I have not kept you waiting !" with this he clapped his hands and rubbed them together, "My name is Zetler, I am Swiss but I now live in Vienna and visit Salzburg quite often. The culture of these cities is unsurpassed !" Jon thought Zetler reminded him of an excited child in an old man's body.

Zetler then introduced himself to each of his guest, "You, Fraulein, are Annelise and you sir are Jon ! And you must be Drew !" And he shook each of their hands vigorously.

Drew took a sip from his drink "So. You're good with names. Can you tell us why we are here ?"

Zetler smiled at Drew's directness, "So honest and forthright. It is a good characteristic, Drew, but please be patient a little while. Please. Take a seat. Let us talk."

Jon sat next to Annelise on the sofa. Zetler chose to stand and Drew sat in a high back lounge chair that he turned toward the smiling face of the old man.

"Let me share some ideas with you," and with a deep breath he began, "As you know, bodies live and die. They are occupied by a soul which eventually inhabits many bodies. In each life it learns lessons as it moves from one host to another until is reaches perfect harmony and knowledge, a state the Hindus call Nirvana, the wise soul. For some this transition can take many lives, perhaps thousands of years. For others it could be aeons but eventually through fortitude they attain this state. The reward is simple. To join with the divine - rest, peace and contentment, a prize indeed !"

Drew, who had been on the edge of his seat fell back into his chair, "Wow !" He exclaimed, "you're talking about a spiritual advancement !"

"Agreed," Jon said, "but, where do we fit into the equation" and he stared in to the dregs of wine in his glass.

"That is simple, " Zetler continued, "for the past few weeks you have been contacted by your spirit guides. Normally these communications are indirect via objects or emotions, sometimes they are through visions of the past or voices or perhaps manifestations. However these voices have been appropriating your dreams, your spirit guides have found it necessary to speak to you directly. You have been set tasks, which so far have been completed admirably." Zetler summarised his thoughts, "You are your spirit guides' representatives on earth and they need you."

"What do mean by spirit guides ?" Annelise asked

"The souls, closer to Nirvana, who watch and try to guide your actions on earth." He turned to Jon, "Yours is your brother ! Normally they observe your time on earth, guiding and setting tasks where possible, noting and reporting your progress. In your case, Jon, little brother is watching you !" And he chuckled to himself.

"What is the purpose of these tasks ?" Annelise asked.

"To prove you are not as insane as some of you were beginning to believe and so help you on the path which leads to who knows where." Zetler replied.

"And your part in this ?" Annelise prompted.

"I have been sent back as an earthly guide of my own volition. To help souls gather their experiences and learn their lessons in more direct ways. In this case I am here to help those who are held by the power of the past and the ones caught in the *Wait State*."

"The Wait State ?" Drew said, "sounds like New York !"

"Droll but sadly incorrect ! The Wait State is the period between death and the next life. When a body dies, there is, by necessity, a period between death and the next life, if it is deemed that there will be a next one. They are held in this 'limbo' to be given time to reflect on their time on earth, their previous lives and to decide on their future. For some souls it will mean returning to earth lower on the spiritual ladder given another chance to learn a lesson or perhaps view their flaws from another perspective. For most it means progression up this ladder."

Zetler leaned against the heater warming his hands and continued," There are still others who are locked into this period by the power of evil on earth, or their own stubbornness, or by an injustice not repaired on earth. It is some of these souls, including your own spirit guides, which you must help gain release from this limbo."

"Are these souls angry ? In pain ?" Annelise asked.

"No. Certainly not in an earthly sense," Zetler was emphatic, "there is no evil in the next world, good always triumphs but anger can manifest itself, in the way an object may be hurled across a room, due to the anguish or injustice of death."

"Are you saying these souls are preparing for reincarnation ?" Drew said sceptically.

"Can it be you do not believe !" Zetler said in mock surprise "well, we shall see in time. The faithless are, after all, a lesson to the faithful. Drew, there are many lives, many dimensions and an infinite number of lives and possible futures. This you will learn. "

Zetler noticed his guests tiring. It would have been a long day for them, "tomorrow we must leave Salzburg. It is our destiny to travel to Scotland to fulfil certain elements of your possible futures, " then he added enigmatically, "on the way we must stop overnight in Stuttgart, there is someone I would like you to meet !"

Zetler then bade each of his guests a good night and organised a taxi for them back to their hotels. Jon thanked Zetler but elected to walk back to the hotel. The city was quiet except for a few couples who were enjoying the romance of the city sparkling with bright lights which illuminated the castle and the cathedral.

Jon stared to the heavens. The night was crystal clear and even with the orange light pollution glow of the city he could see the Milky Way. Staring at the band of stars stretching farther than the imagination Jon felt insignificant. He also felt like a pawn in a complex celestial chess game.

Jon arrived back at his hotel tired and drained but decided to wind down in the bar and ordered an Irish coffee. Sitting at table in the corner was someone he recognised instantly, his attention had been drawn unconsciously by her heavy, clinging perfume.

She looked at him and smiled, "Now. How did I know you were going to be here ?"

"I was going to ask you the same question." Jon said sardonically.

"You are so predictable ! I know what you're going to do before you do it. You're and your friends are going to follow that old fool aren't you ?"

Jon stared into his coffee. She was right of course. "Tell me. Who in the name of Hades are you ?" He asked more in frustration than curiosity.

"Strange how you so aptly asked that question !" She replied sipping her Tequila. Jon watched as the worm turned lazily in the bottom of the glass. The waiter placed Jon's Irish coffee on the table next to him. She smiled at him in self satisfaction. She knew he desired her and Jon knew this himself but, since their last meeting and the many bridges he had crossed he was suspicious of her. He felt he was being manipulated.

"Why are you here ? Have you come to stop us ?" Jon asked.

"No !" she said calmly, "I could not hope to do that but the person who sent me could, he wields unimaginable power. He sent me to uncover your plans and to persuade you to break off from them. You have no hope of success."

"If that were the case, you would not have been sent !" He replied with a smile.

"That is true, but your success would be fatal and of little consequence. You and your friends are merely a distraction."

"Why are you telling me this ?" Jon said.

The woman thought for a moment and said, "I'm taking a great risk here Jon," and she shook head realising that what they once had was buried deep, "you don't remember me do you, Jon ?"

Jon was convinced that they had met. "Was it at school ? College ?"

She smiled, "well in a manner of speaking ! We go back much further. We have loved each other many times."

He felt himself drawn to her but something in his heart resisted. Maybe it was his conscience, maybe the love he had for his wife. In that moment he realised the woman was part of his past but was not to be trusted - cold like the dead creature in her glass. He thought of his wife and he wished that she was there with him. He closed his eyes and could feel her hair, the warmth of her body and the smell of her perfume sweet and warm.

He opened his eyes to see the woman staring at him, "I'm sorry," he said draining his glass in an act of finality, "what must be done will be done. We will maybe set the records straight and perhaps make people look at things differently. What do you care !" He slammed the glass down on the coffee table, got up and went to his room.

She shrugged her shoulders and took another sip of the Tequila and as he walked out of earshot she said under her breath, "I really don't...."

* * * * *

Drew and Annelise slept soundly but, in their sleep, through a shared dream, they were together.

It was a dream of passionate, close, holding, touching, kissing, caressing, a dream of intensity and warmth.

It was a dream of love, of past lives and their own eternal love stretching back to Pagan times.

They saw images from the times of the Romans - a warm villa pool, the era of chivalry - a castle tower of gold, the period of the Cavaliers - a deep quilted four poster bed, the age of Victorians - a summerhouse and the Second World War - a picture house.

They drifted past scenes of their births, marriages, deaths, children, parents, friends and recurring adversaries and they saw how they lives had been good and full of high hopes.

Their lives had simply been a stop over on a long journey, a quest through time to seek themselves.

They saw that through the love and the chaos of the past there was an order.

Things can not be undone but can be redone, they can be repaired whether it was a trial or vicissitude, a barrier or an obstacle. Each new problem was simply another challenge and opportunity.

Was it all that simple ? Just lessons to learn, a few tests to pass, filling in the pieces in a multi-dimensional jigsaw puzzle ?

Annelise and Drew slept and dreamt as one, a warm breath of wind blowing away the cobwebs of their pasts in the darkness of another short night .

They dreamt of a constellation of bright blue light many thousands of light years. It was a place from a long forgotten memory. A place of paradise - the Pleiades...

* * * * *

New York

8th December 1980

The weak sun of a New York winter threw dancing shadows of the trees onto the path. He looked up at the oaks and elms of the park and to the apartment blocks beyond.

He had come to adore New York. His homeland had forgotten his achievements and considered him and his wife undesirables. For his part, he had thumbed a nose at the authoritarians and those empty headed cynics. In New York, however, he and his love could live in peace and outside the limelight they so abhorred.

As they crossed the park they talked about the new album and how it progressed. They felt it was going to be the threshold of a new artistic acceptance. His wife gave him an encouraging squeeze and kissed him on the cheek.

They arrived outside the apartment block and decided to walk past the iron gates to the side entrance rather than use the front door.

They were just about to enter the apartment block when his attention was drawn by a soft voice behind him, "Mr Lennon ?"

He turned, "Yes ?"

He felt something hit his body like a mallet.

And again. And again. And again. And again.

And time stood still...Slowly, like a rag doll he fell.

He hit the ground.

Why ? Drifting. Feeling Heavy. Tired. Time. Not Enough.

In those last moments he heard the music of beauty and peace and with a last breath, he smiled.

That was it !

It was a smile of contentment and triumph !

* * * * *

Reader !

As we flick through the channels on the TV searching for an answer to life and death we are faced with images of sadness, of courage, of cruelty and of strength. We see men and women dying protecting their nearest and dearest, laying down their lives for a greater good. We see men and women dying in horrific circumstances either due to apathy, politics, religion and greed. We see men and women dying for no reason other than to end their torment.

We see death on an oil platform through apathy, we see death in an air crash through greed and watch impotently the genocide of a population that is no more than a thousand miles from our homes.

But, how can the people of power, the movers and shakers, those of influence sleep soundly at night ?

How can these same people go about their daily business without contemplating the torture and torment they bring ?

How will these people reach that higher spiritual ground ?

How will these people hope to redeem themselves ?

Do they not remember their pasts ?

Chapter 13

Turning to Return

"How often do we begin the journey home with sadness not realising when we began our journeys we were already on the homeward way. Life holds the same message ! The day we are born we begin our journeys to the next plane."

Jarrat Toldon - Chronicles of the Future

"Big money goes around the world, big money takes a cruise,
Big money leave a mighty wake, big money leaves a bruise !"

Neil Peart

*I*t was early in the morning when the Espace pulled up outside Jon's hotel. He had been sent a message by Zetler to pack, have breakfast and be ready to leave by eight - he found with surprise that his bill had been paid for him. He felt a slight twinge of sadness as he heaved his luggage into the boot, placing the sword in its box on the top.

Drew and Annelise sat in adjacent seats and Jon chose to sit in the front with Zetler who was to drive. Zetler took a scenic route across the bridges, through the city centre and onto the by-pass with the Hohensalzburg, like a stage set, the magnificent backdrop. Mist and cloud swirled around the summit of the Untersberg and it faded in the rear view mirror as they swept along the quiet autobahn and crossed the open border to Germany.

The mood was sombre and Zetler was the first to speak. "You all slept well ?" he asked and they nodded in agreement. "Sweet dreams ?" He asked and glanced in the rear view at Annelise and Drew who were looking out of the windows.

"Yeah. Sure." Drew said hesitantly wondering if Zetler had some way of viewing his dreams.

"Well, let me do the driving and you relax. Our destination today is a village to the south of Stuttgart, as you know Annelise, only a few hours away. We have to pay a visit on some friends of mine."

Zetler took a tape from the dashboard shelf and slotted it into the cassette player. The machine clicked into operation and took up the leader tape.

"Enjoy the view and enjoy the music !" Zetler said as the first choral and triumphant notes of Vangelis washed from the speakers. Somehow the music matched the vista of the low alpine countryside of Southern Germany perfectly.

With the gentle but continuous sound of the road noise Jon felt relaxed and within half an hour, though he had struggled against it, he had fallen asleep.

The car drove over a small pot hole and Jon awoke with a start. He gathered his senses and looking at his watch realised he had been asleep for over an hour. In the back Drew and Annelise were deep in conversation discussing their journey and studying the maps and guide books strategically placed by Zetler to attract their interest.

Suddenly and without warning Zetler swerved violently from the outside to the inside lane. Instinctively Drew, Annelise and Jon grabbed their arm rests and braced for some impending impact, their hearts skipping a beat.

In the outside lane to the side of them, almost parallel but behind them now, they heard the screech of brakes and the crunch of a collision and then another louder impact.

Jon turned around to see vehicles careering into the hard shoulder, the crash barrier and other cars. His adrenaline flowed as he realised a few seconds earlier they could have been part of it. In the back seats Annelise realised she was gripping Drew's hand for reassurance.

Jon looked at Zetler who relaxed back in his seat continuing his straight course and regaining his concentration as if nothing had occurred.

Jon knew Zetler had reacted seconds before the incident had occurred and had averted their involvement and potential injury.

It was as if Zetler knew something was about to happen.

"Another tape Jon ?" Zetler asked.

* * * * *

The hotel bar was writhing with Friday night celebrations, most of which seemed to involve the young "suits" getting drunk in celebration of the end of another boring but highly paid week.

Ranulf watched one of the men hanging around the neck of a young female colleague.

"Pathetic !" Ranulf thought.

He shook his head in disgust and continued to enjoy his glass of fine malt.

Greed was in the air, a smell so lustful it pervaded the atmosphere surrounding man since those early days of survival on the plains.

Ranulf desired things too.

He desired a woman he could never have and a life full of happiness that could never be granted. Most of all he wanted revenge on the perpetrators of his misery. He would block and torment them every step of his way. He would give them no quarter.

He intended to recover the things that they had stolen from him; Mozart's "Glorianna", da Vinci's earliest notebooks, the lost plays by Shakespeare. They were his and would be his again given time and patience.

He looked around the bar. How could these Plebeians understand the intense pleasure of holding the very parchment that Shakespeare had written on, touch the very pages on which Mozart had doodled, run ones' fingers over the print and inkspots of an imperfect genius !

Was he any different to the rich men who locked their Monet's and Picasso's in bank vaults and safes ?

He smiled again into his glass and sensed someone sitting opposite him. It was her. He could smell her heavy perfume. He looked into her piercing eyes.

"So !" She said kissing his cheek, "Are you going to just stare at that whiskey all night or are you going to buy me a Tequila ?"

* * * * *

1045, Richard Creek Blvd,
Denver, Colorado

29th September

Attention :   The Editor(s)
New York Times
Washington Post
The Times
Die Welt

Sirs,

Reference : Assassination of John F Kennedy, 22nd November 1963

Today I celebrate my 70th birthday. I have lived a full and active life but for some years I have shouldered what has become a heavy burden which today I have chosen to purge from my soul.

During the sixties I was assigned to the CIA Special Service Bureau. This office was controlled and financed from the highest level.

Early in October of 1963 I was assigned the role of "...*the execution of a traitor of the United States...*" and was also designated two other marksmen of the highest calibre. Our task was to assassinate our own President, a task we could not have refused; It was made clear to us that refusal would have meant our own termination.

Over thirty years later and my two associates have long since departed this world. The first died in the first year of the Vietnam war and the second died some months ago from a brain tumour. I have lived in isolation and am therefore the last that can ensure our mission comes to the attention of the American people and the world as it should.

We were positioned in three strategic locations around Deeley Plaza. One close to the railroad sidings behind the so called picket fence, the second high on the building adjacent to the Texas Book Depository and myself in a delivery van on the overpass. I do not know who fired the fatal shot, the tips of our cartridges were designed to do maximum damage on impact, however with this knowledge it will be possible to prove Attorney Jim Garrison's evidence of a conspiracy.

To corroborate my story I have enclosed the remains of a bullet fired from the rifle that can be found in a safe deposit box at the Bank of America in Denver City. You will find the bullet matches the ballistics of this rifle and the bullets that murdered the President and injured the Governor.

Perhaps, in time, the nation can forgive itself for these actions. There can be no more deceptions regarding this crime. We can never understand nor realise the true consequences of our actions and indeed what JFK would have achieved had he have lived.

Today I will have lived my three score years and ten. Today I will end my sleepless nights.

God Bless America !

Lt. John J. Dean.

Jon found the journey stimulating and for the first time in ages he found himself writing in his diary. For September 29th he had written :

Ann. It would bring back memories of our time over here as we drive from Salzburg over the Aichlenburg to Stuttgart. The four hour journey did not pass without incident - Zetler showing us his power of future vision - we learnt later the accident had claimed three young lives.

We stopped for lunch in Munich in one of the central bierkellers. How we found our way to it I shall never understand, and Zetler talked the whole journey about immortality.

He said "...we're only immortal for a limited time. !" We are becoming accustomed to his eccentricities and I am becoming strangely attached to him.

He is taking us to a small convalescent home in a village, Nufringen, close to the Schwarzwald. The home is an asylum for the mentally disturbed and I've no idea why we should bother spending some time there. However it is on our way north and so we are indulging our host.

In the middle of a golden Indian summer afternoon Zetler and his wards arrived in the village of Nufringen a small and typical Swabish community with a few local shops, a small bierkeller and huge red roofed farm in its centre.

Their destination was the asylum built on the edge of the village. Zetler had arranged to meet one of his oldest friends Herman Gaier, a psychiatrist who was one of the leading local experts on reincarnation.

The building was modern, light and airy and had open gardens shaded with pine trees that lead down to the edge of the forest where the only sign of security was a low fence that discouraged the inmates from straying from their sanctuary.

The head nurse ushered them into the garden to wait while she and Zetler sought out Gaier. Drew and Annelise sat on one of the benches and took in the cool breeze and warming sun while Jon decided to stretch his legs.

His attention had been drawn to a young man who sat under a tree reading a book, "The Sorrows of Werther". The young man occasionally looked up nervously from his book as if he had seen something in the woods.

Jon introduced himself. "Hallo," he said nervously offering the man a hand to shake, "my name is Jon."

The man looked up and smiled at him quizzically. "Jon ? That's a good name. There was a saint called John. Have you come to visit or are you going to stay with us ?"

His English was good and Jon decided he was well educated. Jon stared down into the haggard, lined, unshaven face and watery eyes of a man who was perhaps in his mid thirties, about the same age as himself.

"Yes," said Jon as the man closed his book, keeping a finger in the text to mark his spot and glanced again towards the tree line. Jon continued, "my friends and I are here visiting the Herr Doktor Gaier..."

The man was silent for some moments, as if he hadn't heard what Jon had said, then gently grabbing Jon's jacket lapel, pulled Jon closer to him whispering, "You do know he's waiting for all of us don't you ?" He said gesturing toward the forest, "out there !"

"Who is waiting for us ?" Jon asked looked toward where the man stared with increasing agitation.

The young man turned to face Jon, his eyes widening with terror.

He grabbed Jon's lapels tightly and said, "he who will one day take us all away. Be on your guard, Jon. Use the weapon they have given you well. If you don't he may take us all !" And with this cryptic warning the man released his grip and walked nervously back to the main complex.

"There but for the grace of God go I" thought Jon sympathetically.

Strangely the young man was thinking exactly the same thing.

Chapter 14

Past Times

"Time and time again we return to this earth not recognising our pasts. We will sometimes stumble blindly across them and are struck with a strange feeling of recognition of being before, so called 'deja vu' not realising that being able to harness that power would give us the ability to pick up the threads of previous existence and continue our tasks as if the we had never departed."

Jarrat Toldon - Chronicles of the Future

"There isn't a mountain in this whole world that hasn't been climbed."

Steve Hogarth

Nufringen Krankenhaus

*J*on, Drew and Annelise sat patiently in the meeting room waiting for Zetler and Doktor Gaier to arrive. As they approached they could hear their laughter echoing down the corridor. Gaier was a giant bear of a man over two metres tall and with a good humoured and caring face. He greeted them with warm handshakes and apologies for his delay offering them more coffee.

Zetler indicated that his friend should sit down and then took a seat with his back to the window so the sun would warm his back.

Gaier's voice was deep and he spoke in broken English, "My old friend here," he said smiling and indicating Zetler, "tells me that you are interested in," and he thought deeply, searching for the right word, "reincarnation." He continued, "I have a question for you. Which one of you has experienced the sense of belonging or deja vu as it is sometimes known ?"

Jon was about to reply and Gaier smiled holding a hand up to stop him, "My question was rhetorical. You will all have felt it. We have all felt it" and he pointed to Zetler and himself, "but you did not recognise it. Let me shares some ideas with you," and he made himself comfortable in the chair that seemed too small for him.

"The proof of reincarnation is within that feeling. Here at this place I have seen many instances of patients realising their previous lives. This tends to occur under trauma or hypnosis," and he glanced at Drew.

"Within the limited bounds of our Western cultures we still believe that reincarnation is nonsense. Our arrogance demands scientific truth ! The less civilised but more open minded cultures have their very societies built on the concept of returning again and again. American Indians believe in reincarnation, a belief was possibly transmuted from Asia when America and Asia were one land mass but, reincarnation is very strong in Eastern cultures and religions. For example, the Hindu God Shiva represents this cycle of life."

"We have seen how the trauma of death is remembered in the next 'life', when death is so sudden or violent that a phobia occurs in the next existence. One example could be, a death by drowning in one life, may cause a fear of water in the next, normally these phobias are buried in the early years of life. Next, we can observe reincarnation through rebirth experiences, so strong a subject can identify their former home, wife and family through their latent memories. Finally we have seen a body in a new life bearing the marks of death in a previous, for example a birthmark where a bullet entered."

"Western societies rationalise that a child is made of just two genetic elements, it's father and mother. However there is a third, that of the spirit force, the soul. Whereas a body starts to die at birth the soul lives on becoming more complex, gathering experiences from former lives," Gaier turned to Drew, "but, we shall see an example of this today."

The blinds were lowered and Drew settled apprehensively in his chair, he placed his hands on the arm rests and relaxed.

Gaier sat opposite him, "take a deep breath and relax. Take a deep breath and relax." As he repeated this phrase Drew stared into the gently swaying turquoise amulet on a silver chain. Jon and Annelise watched as Drew's breathing became shallower and within moments he was under.

"Drew. We are going to take a journey to a previous incarnation of yours." and Drew's head nodded. "Drew. I want you to tell me where you are...."

Drew's voice sluggishly, almost drunk spoke, "Its hot. I'm in a big black car. There's a crowd. My wife is next to me. The crowd are waving. Damn, it's hot," and Drew seemed to loosen his shirt collar, "they're waving to us, cheering. It's a beautiful sunny day. There are thousands of people."

Gaier waited for Drew to finish, "and what are you doing ?"

Drew took a breath, "I'm waving to the crowd. Smiling. I am holding my wife's hand. I can smell her perfume. I feel happy." Drew was silent for a moment, then his face contorted. Suddenly his hand clutched his throat and he shrieked, "No !!!"

And his vision appeared to him in slow motion...

Hot.

Crowd.

Waving.

Cheering.

Hot.

Sun.

People

Waving.

Smiling.

Perfume.

Happiness.

Perfume.

Crack Bang

Blood.   Neck.   Stop the Blood.

Crack Crack   Bang

Blood.   Pain.   Back.   God.   No.   Not Yet.   Stop the Blood.

Crack   Bang

Silence.

Gaier held Drew's left hand, "What is it Drew ? What's happening ?"

Drew's face was creased and frowning as if he was in great pain, "No," he still clutched his neck, "Got to stop the blood ! No ! Help me ! Another shot."

Jon and Annelise watched with concern as Gaier lead Drew through the painful ordeal. Drew's face was filled with disbelief.

Suddenly Drew twisted and lurched in the seat as if kicked violently in the back, "No ! The pain ! No, please no ! Not yet ! Jesus Christ ! No ! They'll kill us all..."

Then something threw Drew backwards and then forward in his seat and he was silent. He was slumped over on his left side. He looked exhausted, lifeless and inert.

Gaier spoke calmly, "Drew ? Drew ? Can you hear me ? Drew ?" But there was no reply.

Gaier reached out and touched Drew's neck checking for a pulse. It was shallow and barely there and his whole body was drenched with sweat.

Peering closer at Drew's head Gaier noticed something and took out his pen light to examine it. There under Drew's hairline at the back of his head was a large dark red birth mark.

Gaier and Jon lifted Drew from the chair and laid his heavy weight on the couch. Annelise opened the blinds and Zetler poured some coffee.

Gaier sat beside him and spoke with command, "Drew ! When I place my hand on your right cheek you will wake !"

Drew stirred. He mumbled what to Jon sounded like, "They'll kill us all." Drew opened his eyes and closed them again because of the light now streaming through the windows.

He gradually opened his eyes and tried to get his bearings. With a squint he was more audible, "I feel like shit..." He said licking his dry parched lips.

Gaier and Zetler glanced at each other and everyone breathed a sigh of relief. Zetler said, "It seems our American friend has returned to us again !"

Drew sat up and spoke, "My tongue tastes like tin." He rubbed his neck, "so how did I do ? Did anything happen ? Who was I ?"

"Well Drew," Gaier said looking across to Zetler and trying to find suitable words, "have you ever been to Dallas ?"

Stuttgart Neckarhalle

Marcus picked up his old battered Fender guitar by the neck. He felt a gentle push in the small of his back, his cue to go on stage. The concert, his first in a hall of this size, had been beyond belief. Tonight he had realised all his hard work and sacrifices had been rewarded. His fans had adored it and he had one more gift for them. Stalking through the gloom he saw the hall was illuminated dimly with thousands of flecks of light as his followers lit matches or lighters to brighten the darkness like fireflies twinkling in the black.

He stepped onto his mark and immediately on cue he was lit with pencil beams of silver light that focused on his guitar. The crowd greeted it with euphoria, cheering and chanting their litany. He had promised them a new song and this one was special. It had come to him in a dream and had rung in his head for days. He knew they would appreciate it.

His fingers found the first note and his foot touched the guitar pedal. He closed his eyes and the guitar rang out a single screaming note like a banshee. It was a note so powerful you felt like putting hands to your ears. It rang around the hall echoing and reverberating back to him. He pushed the pedal forcing more from it and the note screamed on in anguish as he wrung it from the instrument. It was not a single sound but a complex interwoven mix of harmonies and variations around one note.

The crowd were silent and transfixed, as the same note was picked up from the keyboards behind with a choral harmony. The bass pedal growled and droned then the drum beat began strong, straight and true. His fans adored it, but it was impossible not to enjoy the "Perfect Note", the title he had given it.

That night was the threshold of a new era. It was the last night that he was in control, the beginning of the end, thrown on the roller coaster which over the years sapped his will and creativity and led him relentlessly toward self destruction. The piece was released as a single staying Number 1 for 15 weeks, the album became best selling of the year and stayed in the charts for three years following its release and only knocked from the top spot by Marcus' follow up album.

Four years after writing the "Perfect Note" at the Wembley Stadium on the final date of his "Perfect World Tour" an hour after the concert Marcus committed suicide. He was 32, unmarried with no children. His entire estate was donated to charity. One of his requests was that a foundation to promote music be established in his home town and that he should be buried in its grounds. On his headstone, visited in pilgrimage by his followers, were carved his dates and the epitaph :

May You Make Your Dreams Last Longer than a Night.

Grindelwald, Switzerland

High on the mountain she could hear the trains clattering up gradients that even a mountain goat would balk at. The view from the terrace with the valley spread out below her was so magnificent it took her breath away. She had been there most of the day breathing air so fresh it made her feel almost drunk. Her asthma during the last two years had got progressively worse, London life was fast but had shortened her life. It had become unbearable and she had quit her job, begun to write and had moved to Switzerland where, high on the hills she could breathe again.

That had been six months ago and the summer was almost over. The snow was beginning to fall and her Swiss dream was turning from meadow green to white. At the end of these days she felt content and lethargic. Her notepad was beside her containing the notes she needed to attain her new goal.

One night she had had a dream that had changed her life reminding her of the days she spent as a child with her parents in Switzerland. It had given her the longing to return and the impetus to change her lifestyle. Her boyfriend of some years had been shocked, not to say devastated. Her decision to resign her job and use her savings to travel to and then perhaps eventually settle in Switzerland was absolute. She was determined not to drift through life and she had not regretted it. She felt to write a novel was a catharsis, a cleansing of the soul and Switzerland was renewing her body. She felt whole again, independent, motivated and filled with new life.

She settled back in her chair sipping her wine and took in the spectacular vista. The day was fading and clouds gathered around the Eiger peak, its north face scarred with snow, cragged and harsh, foreboding as legend had made it. Along the ridge the dirty white glacier moved imperceptibly.

Below her she could hear laughter some miles away of someone enjoying the summer evening. Crickets chirped and birds sang sleepily. Street lights in the village and night lights in far off chalets twinkled on. On the Pfinstegg the cable car was silent and flags hung limp in the lifeless air. The church tower pointed to the first evening star while the clock struck nine. She shivered and wrapping her cardigan around herself returned indoors to the hotel fire for warmth and a hot chocolate before bed.

The bar was deserted except for her future husband sitting at the bar reading a map and sipping a beer. She acknowledged him with a faint smile and he nodded and made a brief comment about the coolness of the evening air.

It is extraordinary how fate attempts to camouflages itself, for in that brief faint smile were new roads, new experiences and a new life !

Chapter 15

Ripples

"We realised late in our development that the physical laws of each action having an equal an opposite reaction hold true throughout the cosmos, having no concept of the holistic nature of our world. One man's smallest action causes ripples that wash through time and space and effect the outcome of every decision made in the cosmos. Sometimes these causes are minute. Sometimes they are catastrophic !"

Jarrat Toldon - Chronicles of the Future

"Sail away, away. Ripples never come back."

Mike Rutherford

During the afternoon Drew became stronger and felt happier to talk about his experience. His regression under hypnosis had revealed a connection in his past of which even Zetler and Gaier had not conceived. Drew had relived JFK's assassination as if he had been there, either Drew had been JFK or had a strong connection to what was once JFK. Both possibilities were to be explored.

After farewells, the group loaded back into the Espace and drove from the asylum. In a window overlooking the drive the young man with whom Jon had spoken looked up from his book and waved unemotionally as the car disappeared down the tree-lined lane and out of view.

Gaier decided that they should also visit a hospice in the North of Stuttgart some 30 kilometres away where they cared for the terminally ill. It was managed by one of Gaier's ex-colleagues and he had rung ahead to confirm the visit of Zetler and guests. Many of the patients in the hospice had had near death experiences that Gaier and Zetler thought would strengthen the arguments for proof of an after-life in case any of his group had any doubts.

The traffic around the city was heavy and it took nearly an hour to travel the short distance. Drew seemed to be in a different world, not even talking to Annelise. He stared from the car window at the other drivers taking part in the daily rat race. The materialism and hedonism of his life thus far now seemed futile and hollow. He now realised there were *more things in heaven and earth* than he had dreamed of.

* * * * *

The nurse, crisp white, bleached clean and neat, leaned over the bed and rearranged the pillows. She plumped them into a soft shape to give the patient support.

Daniel's eyes were bloodshot but hardly open. A tear of pain and sorrow crept its way down his cheek. Nurse Elisabeth gripped Daniel's hand in comfort and sat down next to him on the bed. She had seen this many times but it still made her soul twist in anguish, perhaps in an echo of her own future destiny.

"Do you want to talk about it ?" She asked wiping the tear away with a tissue that she took from a pocket in her uniform.

Silence. She tried again. "It's all right. Please let it out." She said reassuring him.

Daniel turned about accusingly. His dim eyes were wide with fear, grief and bitterness. His heart was full of trepidation.

"I'm frightened", he pleaded, "I don't want to die ! Not yet !"

With a surge of energy he wrapped his arms around her, she returned a maternal comforting hug. The nurse patted and stroked his back. Over his shoulder she looked into the garden at the tree swaying in the breeze. She saw the reddened sunshine and the dry autumn leaves blown by the breeze.

"I've seen many like you Daniel," she said shaking her head, "none of them are ever ready."

"But why me ? Why do I...." Daniel turned away.

"Some fight against it with their last drop of strength, but in the end all resign themselves to it. They were all, without exception, frightened of death."

For a few moments there was quiet, peace. The nurse holding his hand, the patient content to accept comfort. Daniel thought of his own short mortality and finally broke the silence, "what will happen to me ?" He asked.

The nurse thought of the many times she had had these conversations and replied as she always did, "you will sleep, rest and awake in a new world" The nurse adjusted the pillows behind him.

"Will I dream ??" He thought for a moment and his nurse realised it was a question that he would answer himself, "I hope so." He said and fell back on the pillows turning toward the russet light of that autumn day.

* * * * *

The nurse stubbed out her cigarette on the ashtray and wafted her hands around her mouth to dissipate the smell. It was strictly forbidden to smoke within the building and the doctor would be here in a moment. She hurriedly took out a mint and crunched it, the visitors would also be here soon.

The hospital smelt hot and bleached clean. As Jon and the others entered they were greeted by Dr Folkes who was accompanied by Head Nurse Trupp who looked pristine in the virgin white uniform, shoes and cap. They exchanged greetings and were ushered into a coffee and rest area with low chairs and melamine round tables.

Dr Folkes started with an introduction, "as you know we care here for the terminally ill. Everyone here has only a few months, weeks, days or hours to live and we try to make their final days as calm, untraumatic and painless as possible. As you might imagine it can be upsetting and our nurses rarely accustom themselves to the task. Each patient has a private room, often the best for the last few days where the patient eventually comes to terms, at least superficially, with the inevitable."

"Do your patients sometimes die," and Drew searched for the right words, "with any animosity or anger for their situation ?"

"Sometimes, though this is very rare. After all they do not really have the strength to, most tend to just drift away." Folkes replied.

"How do you prepare them for their deaths ?" Annelise said

"We try to put them at ease, talk about how we know it to be painless and pleasant. It comforts them to know that there is a next world." The nurse replied.

Jon looked perplexed, "but, how can you tell them of the next world when you can not be sure of its existence ?"

"We've seen a number who have drifted in and out of death. Some of them come back because they have unfinished business or want to say farewell to their family or friends in this world. Those who have returned describe a variety of experiences and these tend to share a common theme." she replied

Drew sat forward, fired with interest.

Dr Folkes continued, "their stories often begin with a sense of floating above their beds out from their bodies. They feel as if they are rising, leaving the earth behind. They talk of flying, floating through the ceiling and speak of a warm joyous feeling and a blinding white light. Some mention a spirit guide leading them along a glowing tunnel. Some talk of the stars."

He stirred his luke warm coffee, "all of them talk of being given a choice and deciding to return. They drift away from this dimension and arrive in an idyllic paradisian world. But let me allow one of our more perceptive patients to explain this to you, her name is Frau Dauber."

They walked from the rest area to a row of private wards that were luxurious with comfortable chairs, television, telephone and music centres. After the usual formalities of greeting and a frantic search for other chairs with Jon sitting on the bottom of the bed the interview began.

"Frau Dauber," the doctor paused, "we've been discussing your case and what you say took place during your cardiac arrest two weeks ago. Could you tell us a little about the experience."

"Certainly." Frau Dauber took a sip of water from the glass on the bed side table. "I have never been fit. As you can see I have often eaten too much and my health is not good. I was admitted three weeks ago after feeling faint at work. Once admitted, I was to have a number of tests and was nervous and apprehensive. Then, one minute I was lying here feeling a groggy and the next I was surrounded by commotion."

Dr Folkes interjected, "Frau Dauber had a cardiac arrest and we were alerted by the monitors and alarms."

Frau Dauber continued, "I seemed to have two doctors and four nurses around me. I watched for some moments and then the scene below began to fade. I felt myself rising above it, I felt as if I was flying, I felt so free. I twirled and spun and dived with the energy of a child. Below me I could see the ward, the hospital, the town and the earth shrinking and a long silver thread, a life line snaking below me. Suddenly ahead I could see a bright disk of shining light. As I stared into its centre I felt safe, secure and loved. Then I was moving upwards and felt almost as if I was on a travelator moving along a tunnel. In the distance I saw a figure bathed in light greeting others before me who were being led through various large portals. There was a huge window and I could see the earth turning in the darkness through it. I arrived at this gateway and could see the guide talking to my husband who seemed to be pleading with him. As I arrived my husband approached me and said 'You must return. You have other lessons, other purposes to fulfil. Think of the grandchildren,' and I felt a pang of regret, a tug as if jolted by a rope and found myself waking on the bed."

"Where did you think you had gone to ?" Annelise asked.

"I was in the next world. Paradise, my dear !" Frau Dauber replied.

"I've heard the phenomena called the Near-Death-Experience." The doctor took out a packet of mints and offered them around.

"Certainly according to the equipment, Frau Dauber had died. She had been dead for over two minutes, she should have been brain damaged. Our instruments showed no life, no activity. However, just before she awoke the dials went crazy."

"Have you ever known cases like this before ? Surely this is a rarity." Drew asked.

"It is by no means a rarity ! We have such incidents many times a month, they are becoming more common place as our technology cheats death."

Annelise turned to Frau Dauber, "what do you think your husband meant by lessons and purposes - think of the grandchildren ?"

"I'm unsure but it could refer to my grandson Kurt. He is a worry and has been in a few scrapes before, but he seems to look to me for guidance. Essentially I feel my work on earth is not yet done, I feel I have a few more years in me yet, a few more lessons to learn ! As I'm sure we all do !"

"Maybe it is a fantasy created by the brain to ease the trauma of death ? Just a chemical chain reaction, the last sparks of a dying flame, like an adrenaline release when under stress." Drew said cynically.

"Maybe the tunnel is a recollection of birth ?" Jon added.

Doctor Folkes frowned shaking his head, "These are by no means isolated incidents ! They happen in every case, reactions and recollections imply a random element but the experiences correspond across lives and even cultures ! They cannot be the actions of a dying mind ! The belief of purposes to fulfil is also very common, as is the belief that their own lessons are not yet finished, that their schooling is not yet over."

"And these stories are always the same ?" Annelise asked

"I've read a variety of descriptions, certainly. As a person dies their whole life may pass before them as a movie or a succession of still pictures. Finally their soul leaves the body and rises above it where they watch the action going on around their detached body . After a short period of what feels like flying, the spirit finds itself in a dark tunnel with a tiny white speck of bright light at end of it. Sometimes this light is like a rainbow and there is a feeling of warmth, love and peace."

As if on cue the sun streamed through the open windows, "The light gets closer and closer until it envelops them. The white light becomes a white door; a gateway. They are finally in a place where relatives, angels and others are there to greet them. The place is like a beautiful garden. It is at this point that they are either told or decide to return."

"You seem to have a personal interest in the stories." Drew said.

"Yes. Some years ago after a car accident the same happened to me. I returned because I heard my wife and children calling me."

"Is there a common last word from your patients ?" Jon asked.

"It's funny. I have often wondered about its significance. They often mention home. For example *I am home* or *I am almost home.*"

There was a pregnant silence as the group took in this information. It was broken by Zetler who looked at his watch and announced that they must depart.

The nurse showed the visitors back to the reception area and she watched them leave. It was funny, one of them seemed very familiar and reminded her of someone. Maybe it was when she worked in the hospice in England and she remembered Daniel, the tearful young man that she had held in her arms.

* * * * *

The light was bright.   So white and bright.

He could hear two voices and the trees, he enjoyed the sound of the wind blowing gently through the trees.

He felt so tired and the pain was now no more than a dull ache.

He thought.   Yes.   It was time.

And he took a final deep breath.....

* * * * *

The group finally arrived at the hotel late in the evening. It had been a long day and Annelise went straight to her bed. She felt very strange staying in the hotel that she passed every day on her way to work. Jon, Drew and Zetler, meanwhile, had decided to end the day with a hot Irish coffee and a game of chess.

Zetler sat at the bar viewing his two wards as a shepherd watches his sheep. Jon and Drew set up the pieces and began the game. After fifteen or so moves the game slowed and Jon looked under pressure.

He thought pensively about his next move. He thought about its consequences. He thought about alternatives. He thought about different paths to the same goal. He thought of defeat. He thought about his adversary. He thought about his future.

Jon realised that the game was a microcosm of life. It represented sacrifice, war, futility, protection, chivalry, power, weakness, life and death. He realised that his decision to take a piece sent ripples around the board that might lead to the elimination and removal of a piece.

Maybe this was the lesson he was to learn, the interconnectedness of lives, the holistic nature of the world, the link between action and consequence.

Meanwhile Drew had taken out the old ivory chess piece from his jacket pocket and held it in his hand, nursing it as he had done many times throughout the journey.

The chess piece had travelled many miles in its lifetime, almost circumnavigating the globe as its original owner had done ten centuries before. It had travelled ever westward, from generation to generation, from culture to culture, until it was on the final 1000 miles of its journey home.

Drew held it up to the light over the bar and examined its carving and the skill that had gone into making it. His fingers ran over the crown and bearded face of the king tracing the folds in the cloak. The chess piece had been caressed and held so many times before on its journey by the leaders of many cultures through those ten centuries. All had recognised its beauty but none of them had realised its significance.

He placed it next to the board as if to allow it to observe the action. Jon made his move and picked up his knight and took Drew's bishop.

"Not bad old buddy. Not bad," Drew reach over and removed Jon's knight with a pawn placing it beside the old chess piece. The diagonal movement of the pawn exposed the rank and empty space between Drew's queen and Jon's king, "and check !" He added with a smile.

London

Spring 1990

The auction room was packed, it was a very popular event. Anxious faces scanned curled-up catalogues to see what the next lot would be. It was all part of the excitement, guess the price and perhaps pick up a bargain. The next item was called; "Lot 129. A silver cigarette case made in Dublin in 1909 engraved with initials E.M."

It was held aloft on a burgundy velvet cushion for all to see. The auctioneer continued:

"The original owner is believed to have been a third class passenger. Found in the debris field in the first expedition of 1985. Exhibited with items from the wreck in London at the National Maritime Museum and now to be sold to raise funds for future exhibition projects. Can I open the bidding at £100 ?"

The bidding was brisk and Ranulf marvelled as the price rose steeply. For something that had no intrinsic value - possibly £100 - to be sold at 5 or 6 times its value seemed ludicrous to him. He had already watched china vegetable dishes being snapped up for £100 each - ridiculous ! Still, what was money to him ?

For him the cigarette case was not simply a bizarre link to a disaster that had claimed some 1500 lives. To him the item was a vital key, a powerful link in the chain of events that he sought to perpetuate and without which would probably destroy him.

The bids had begun to rise more slowly. It was currently at £600. Ranulf grinned to himself and knew that now it was time, "six hundred and sixty-six pounds !" He said smiling wickedly into his catalogue.

The audience murmured at the strange bid and turned to examine the bidder. Ranulf gazed unemotionally at the auctioneer and shrugged. He knew no one was going to better the price.

"Going once." Silence as the auctioneer scanned the room, "going twice," no opposing bid. "Sold to the gentleman at the back. Thank you sir."

Ranulf had another piece to lock away safely in his collection. He held all the trump cards. Surely they were powerless now . The dark haired woman accompanying him closed her catalogue, "well Ranulf ? Are you happy ?"

Ranulf smiled smugly. Happy was not the word. Avenged was more apt.

Chapter 16.

Sins of the Fathers

"There is a Taoist proverb which states 'going on means going far, going far means returning'. If this is true and we do always return to our points of embarkation why then do we journey at all ? Is the experience worth it ? The reason is simple ! How can we know ourselves without knowing others."

Jarrat Toldon - Chronicles of the Future

"One man's joy makes another man weep,
Nothing you can do is ever going to change it
One man's saint is another man's fool, One man's hot is another man's cool !"

Genesis

T he gentle movement of the car had sent Jon to sleep. He awoke to the sound of voices and a new voice in particular.

"Yeah ! I'm on the way to London. It's where the action is. There's some march there and I'm meeting a friend. He says he's going to show me the sights !"

The voice belonged to a student dressed in a worn combat jacket, jeans and a tee-shirt, his rucksack lay next to him. "You guys ever been to Amsterdam ? he asked. "They say hash is really cheap !"

Jon had never understood the desire to take drugs. Getting high on anything even as "soft" as cigarettes or alcohol seemed a pointless pastime. It seemed to him that whatever goes up must eventually come down. He gradually opened his eyes and they grew more accustomed to the light again. He looked out of the car and saw they were passing through the Moselle Valley with the route flanked by wineries and acres of vineyards.

"Wow man ! There's a few good parties to be had on those hills," the student nudged Jon and tried to imagine how many bottles of wine they would produce.

Jon sat up deciding to be sociable, "Where are you at University ?"

The man laughed, "used to be ! Used to be ! Things got too heavy. Decided all I wanted to do is travel. See the world. I was down in Munich seeing my girlfriend. She wanted to come too but I need the freedom."

115

Jon smiled, a little envious of this free spirit, "you're lucky."

"Right on, man ! I don't want any hassles; just wanna breath !"

"When you've finished travelling what are you going to do ?" Jon asked guessing the answer.

"It's a big world you know and I'm not getting any younger. I just want to see it all first," and he smiled to himself and stared out across the valley.

At the next service area they sat and chatted some more over a cup of strong German coffee. The student scrounged a cigarette from another of the diners and lit it from the candle that tried to make a functional Formica topped table a little more homely.

"Problem is materialism. People always wanting something. Not by need but by desire, a bigger house, a bigger car, better video and better microwave. Choice ! These are man's driving forces and we pour more pressure on an overburdened throw away world. We're sick, man," he shook his head and drew on the cigarette, which was down to its last centimetre.

"See," and the butt was pointed accusingly in Jon's direction, "once people were happy to just to have a place to stay and enough to eat but now the will to live has been replaced by a will to out do. We've forgotten what it really is all about. We are manipulated by big business and governments and encouraged to live beyond our means by a lust to have something we don't really need, can't really afford and could well do without. Instead of winners we are becoming losers."

He thought for a while and looked across the car park as a Mercedes turned into a tight parking spot, "and the world gets sicker and our civilisations decline. The atmosphere becomes unbreathable and we punch a bigger hole through it. When will it end ? When some thoughtless bastard crosses one too many lines and blows the ass off the world."

He brushed the lank hair from his face and stubbed out what was left of his cigarette. His face was full of sadness, "so many lives. So many broken hearts. So many lost souls and all for some elusive pot of shit at the end of a fading rainbow."

Eventually they arrived at Zeebrugge where they were to take the crossing to Dover. They dropped the hitch hiker at the docks where he could pick up a lift and Zetler decided it was probably better to get a good nights rest in preparation for the English traffic they would face the next day.

The hotel was of the generic and functional type that, though comfortable, gave no clue as to what continent, country or city you were in. They agreed to meet, after freshening up, in a private conference room which Zetler had managed to arrange at short notice. Half an hour later they were sat around a large teak table laid out with glasses and orange juice for a business meeting. Notepad and pencils had been provided and Drew had already decided to fill up the empty space of the front sheet with bizarre doodles.

Zetler stood up and clasping his hands in front of him said, "I want to tell you a story that concerns all of you. It concerns genealogy and begins many years before you were born." He took a sip of water.

"There was once a sailor called Njal. He was a young man and quite intelligent for a man of his rank. He played chess. He had learnt the game from his father who himself had learnt it when he had travelled to the East. His father had bequeathed him a valuable set that had been made three centuries earlier by a master craftsman. When the sailor died this set was buried with him - except for one vital piece. That single piece travelled the oceans and was given as a gift to the natives of a New World. After many years the piece eventually came into the possession of Njal's direct ancestor who sits with us as the table this evening."

As Zetler finished the sentence Drew broke from his doodling and took out the piece placing it front of him. He was speechless. Zetler continued.

"There was once a great composer, his music known and loved throughout the world. One of his greatest pieces, some would say his best was a Requiem which was begun near the time of his untimely death and remained unfinished. The last movement was lost apparently dying with Mozart. At the time of Mozart's death a bookseller bought a prayer book. His great love was music. When he opened the back of the book he realised what had come into his possession. He owned the piece of a jigsaw puzzle that had been completed by Mozart's pupil. More importantly, before he could reveal what he had he was murdered and the book was stolen from him. After many years the piece eventually came into the possession of this man's direct descendant. She too sits with us this evening."

Annelise shuffled nervously in her seat. The prayer book she knew was safe in her suitcase.

"Finally, we turn to the third of our stories. Count Orgaz was a lord of the land of Aragon. Orgaz had for some years fought against the infidels and had been renowned in battle. In his right hand he carried a sword, a blade made by the finest craftsmen of Toledo. When he had been slaughtered the sword had been taken from him and for a time was lost until recovered by the son of his ancestors," and he looked directly at Jon.

Vienna

December 1791

That night, it rained in torrents, flooding the streets and turning the country roads into rivers. The carriage clattered over the cobblestones through the darkness and the lanterns gave only crude light making visibility difficult.

The carriage passed through the city gates and out towards the pauper's cemetery. His servant and driver were sworn to secrecy and had agreed to help the Baron in his grim task. The carriage drew up beside the pit and the driver and servant took a lantern each and peered into the pit.

"Can you see it ?" The Baron called through the rain, "is it there ?"

The lanterns shone into the chasm and the dim light made out the forms of the linen body bags in the pit.

"Can you see it ?" The Baron's voice became urgent realising his position if his actions were discovered, "look for the gold thread of the ties."

The lights scanned the pit and suddenly the driver called out, "sir, I can see it. It is there. I can make out the ties quite clearly."

At that the Baron and his servant hurried over holding their lanterns out into the gloom. The servant took a bundle of rope from the knapsack he carried unravelling it from a grappling hook on the end. He threw it into the pit like a macabre fishing game. The rope became taught and the servant and driver hauled on it, dragging the body easily from the mud of the pit. With some trepidation they hauled the body into the carriage laying it on the carriage floor and covering it with a large heavy tapestry.

The journey back into the city was no less treacherous. The guards at the gates waved the carriage and its cargo through without inspection as the Baron expected them to on so wet a night. Within minutes they arrived at the Baron's palatial home where the carriage pulled up at the rear of the house. His family were all in bed and the house was quiet. Hastily the body was recovered from the carriage and bundled unceremoniously down the steps to the family crypt and laid on the altar with the tapestry covering it.

Tomorrow he would arrange for an embalmer to prepare the body properly, one of the brother's could arrange this. Then the body was to be reburied in the safety of the consecrated ground of the Baron's family vault. There it would find rest and would have the same nobility in death as the music that the Baron so admired in life.

* * * * *

It was a windy Sunday morning and Ranulf watched as the peace march made its way into Trafalgar Square for the prearranged rally. Freaks from all over Britain and Europe had descended on the city. Punks, Rastas, NewAgers, no hopers, he loved watching them - pitiful politically correct bastard 2CVer's. Spineless cheesecloth's and sandals plus a liberal sprinkling of social workers. Naive and as stupid as the dumb animal's they sought to protect. Prole pacifists with no idea of where they were going nor what they were going to do when they got there.

Maybe they celebrated, as did the rest of the western world, that the Iron Curtains had been opened and the walls had come down. The folks in the US and the rest of the best of the west thought that now the cold war was over the world was a safer place.

Idiots ! What about the religious fanatics , the nationalists, the radicals, the left wingers, the right wingers, the PLO, IRA, Shining Path, Red Brigade, Saddam, Gaddafi, Castro, the Chinese, the Israelis, de Blank and all the other bloody radicals and lunatics who believe the bomb and the gun speaks louder than the voice. All those power seeking crazies who have an axe to grind and a desire to sink it into some poor defenceless bastard.

With a cry of "God is on our side", that eternal religious battle cry that means a few thousand ordinary cannon fodder folk are about to die.

Why would God be on the side of oppression and obsession ? The continuation of might is right continues the eternal political imbalance. The poor starve and rich get fatter. The banks get richer and the poor get weaker. I guess no one ever thought to ask what God thought of it all !

So. Question. Are all the petty arguments about some piece of desert or some square of land over ? Are they over in the Baltics, the Sudan, the Sinai, Hong Kong, Rwanda, Serbia, the East, the West, the North, the South. Where ever you look there's another battle of ideologies in progress and when can we expect some playground scrap over a few acres of ground to turn into one almighty holocaust. War. Magnitude One. Christ help us ! Give it ten years !

Still the eternally optimistic mankind says the world is a safer place. Mankind's got a long way to go and a lot to learn. They said, "if Jesus were alive today there would never be another bullet fired."

It was comforting to Ranulf that where ever there is man there is evil and wherever there is goodness there is badness. Ranulf turned his face to the wind and walked down Whitehall toward the Thames.

* * * * *

119

Zetler leaned over the table staring intensely at the group, "these objects are part of a jigsaw through time and dimensions. Their loss has caused their owners much grief and their recovery will hopefully save many souls."

He took a deep breath and continued, "Each of the souls exist in torment. Their lives and their destinies were ended before time and their mission was incomplete. The recovery of these pieces is the first step towards their final rest."

He sat back in his chair to complete his story. "This is my final tale. There was once a young man just out of boyhood. His mother was tried, unfairly, as a witch and sentenced. Her death became the stepping stone which led to revenge. Now he is no longer a human but inhuman and is guided by evil. He feeds off life. But, the more he feeds the more he must feed. That is his torment !"

Zetler took a sip of orange juice, "His name is Ranulf and he knows the power of these objects. He has owned each of them for a brief time. However he has captured the souls of those who owned these things - Njal, Orgaz, Hirschfelden and others. They all exist eternally in the Wait State. Thankfully, we now have the power to release them."

Jon's face shone in realisation as he began to understand the last few weeks of his life. Zetler continued, "In releasing them, like a domino effect, we release others. Your brother, for example," and he pointed to Jon, "waits for his mentor who is also held in the Wait State. You, Annelise. Your love waits to be released."

"You have now reached a fork in life's path. It is your time and your choice will decide your future. The path I ask you to choose is the untrod one. You are being asked to fight on the side of good and you will make sacrifices which will give others what they desire most. We have to ask you to make these sacrifices in the names of many whom you have never met, to bring rest to the restless, peace to the tormented and sleep to the ones who wait."

Drew shook his head in disbelief. Zetler continued, "It is our task to close a gateway. It is a gateway over which Ranulf has a great power. Our chances of victory and success are high but the road will be hazardous. In this goal we must be in agreement. We must take a vote. To proceed or to go back."

On another plane three spirits prayed for guidance. Jon, Drew and Annelise looked at each other and nodded in agreement.

"Good !" Zetler said proudly, "I expected no less !"

Chapter 17

The Mirror Always Lies

"It is strange how mankind approaches a challenge. Some stare out impeding disaster, catatonic, as an animal blinded by a bright light. Others are wise enough to reason that there is nothing to fear but fear itself thus resigning themselves never to repeat the same errors of judgement again."

Jarrat Toldon - Chronicles of the Future

"I want to love, I want to give, I want to find another way to live. Another shout, another cry and the walls come tumbling down."

Yes

Jon sat on the deck sheltering from the cold wind that gusted around the ship's stern and made the flag flap furiously. He was pondering the future of the group and could see where they were heading. He believed their purpose to be a creditable one but he could see the danger and he feared it.

Behind him the continent disappeared into the murk appearing to sink into the grey muddy sea. The last two weeks had been a blur, but he seemed able to recall the smallest detail of it as if he was reborn with a purpose.

He knew that the future, his earthly future, was at best, bleak. He realised that somehow he had been marked for some design that he could not totally comprehend and that death stood waiting at the end of it. He was not fearful of death as he knew for sure it could not be oblivion, his brother had demonstrated that, but he did fear the nature of his death and whether it would be painful, slow or quick.

With his hands deep in the pockets he wrapped his coat around himself and felt the bitter chill of the cold sea wind with a hint of autumn in the air.

Resigning himself to his future fate he took out his notebook and a pen and began to write. His was no poet but he could feel the pull of the sea and the rush of the air and the clouds drifting overhead and he wrote a poem, lines that he felt he had to get down. His pen flowed without effort and his thoughts took shape coherently and with form and shape.

Children of the Elements

If the sea were an ally and the wind an old acquaintance

If the sun were a brother and the clouds were old friends

Then the earth would be solid , a rock to cling on to

And our lives just a passing refrain of a song

Still the grass grows no quicker when you watch its unending

Quest for the sunlight upon its short blades

And the clouds rain refreshes and the sun's warmth brings new life

For lives are much brighter than colours that fade

And strong the sea rages like a storm in the summer

Still the sun warms us on the coldest of days

And the clouds pass on over , a passing acquaintance

So the wind blows our dreams to dissolve in the haze

Rhayader, Wales

Autumn 1632

The small boy breaks off his play and hides behind the barn as torches flickering in the night herald the arrival of the mob , calling and shouting to the farmstead, carrying sticks, pitchforks and muskets. The boy is frightened and shrinks further into his hiding place afraid to make a sound. He knows these men; villagers, the fathers of his playtime friends. At their head is a priest, their village priest, respected, stern and uncompromising. Black, sober bigot and burning with the passionate fires of hell and damnation.

The mob break down the flimsy door and enter the farmhouse. There are shouts. A cry from his mother and then a scream. There is pleading, a cry of pain and anguish from his father then a shot. Now, there are many screams, frantic from his mother. The boy cowers lower and begins to sob. Tears wash down his face, rivers on his dirty cheeks. Should he go to help or should he stay hidden, safe from his vantage point ? The men reappear now dragging the woman from the farmhouse which is now ablaze.

"Witch. Heathen. Whore", they cry and taunt her. Why doesn't his father help? Why doesn't he come from the house ? Where has he gone ?

They roughly tie his mother to the barren apple tree in the centre of the farmyard. Suddenly bails of hay and bundles of sticks are brought from the barn and piled around the tree. A torch is put to them and they burn, hesitantly at first then fiercely. The fire burned intensely turning the tree into an inferno. The boy is helpless, he cannot save her. He sobs in fear and helplessness. His mother screams and then is silent. Ranulf turns and runs, running until his legs are lead. After crossing fences and fields he finds himself at his favourite spot by the riverside. He crawls into the den he made last summer and curls up, crying himself to sleep.

"They will pay for this," he sobs hitting the hard cold ground with his fist in the darkness, "They will pay. They will all pay......"

And in that cold crisp darkness the twins, revenge and hatred, were born. Darkness is an uncaring ally. It cloaks the truth and camouflages the wicked. It blankets the light and brings with it fear. At night the truth is poorly lit. At night Ranulf's rage was complete. He knew his enemies were getting closer and he did not fear them - he loathed and detested them.

Above all he hated one in particular. The one whose forefather had spawned the hatred in his heart. He would pay a thousand fold. During the months leading to this moment his possessions had been stolen and plundered. His soul raped and his will to survive pushed to the limits. But, he would not bend, he would not fall, he would recover. He knew that when his enemies were as one they were also at their most vulnerable. When they came together to destroy him that meeting would be their doom.

In the apartment high above the city of London he remembered that night four centuries before. Gazing out of the window over the metropolis he watched the lights. Dusk was falling quickly and the darkness was come again.

Something deep inside his being gripped his heart. He threw open the window and a blast of cold air almost pushed him backwards. He gripped the sides of the window frame and looked down to the streets 50 floors below him. The thought of flying twisted in his mind. Suddenly he screamed at the night like a lone wolf howling at the moon.

"R e v e n g e ! ! !" He screamed in anguish. And just for a moment he thought the city had been silenced by his wailing banshee cry. He took a deep breath and sobbed. Whether it was for war or for peace he knew not.

* * * * *

Some hours later, Zetler and his party had navigated their way around London and had arrived in the heartland of England finding a small Cotswold pub for lunch. Jon was not hungry and decided to explore the village.

Across the green was a village church with a well-tended graveyard with deep green yew trees. Jon decided to have a look inside and lifting the latch pushed open the heavy oak door. The smell of damp, cold and musty hymn books assailed his nose. He walked down the nave gazing up at the simple wooden arches and white plastered ceiling. He chose a pew near the front and absorbed the peace and tranquillity of the moment.

A voice spoke behind him and for a second he did not hear it, "you look deep in thought." The voice was kind and calm and its timbre was comforting. It belonged to a young woman in her early twenties who wore the traditional black habit and white collar of a country vicar.

"Yes !" Jon replied, "enjoying the beauty of your church."

"Yes it is beautiful. God's beauty of course !" She said looking up at the cross over the altar.

"Do you believe God really exists ?" Jon asked uncertainly.

She turned to him, "Of course ! Undoubtedly !" she said, "you can see it in the colours of the day or the crystal clear of a winter's night."

Then, she pointed to the sunshine blazing through the stain glass. "Just imagine that power. Imagine the energy of a billion billion stars. Imagine the force that created them in one cataclysmic explosion. The energy of exploding supernova, dying stars converted into life, the living breathing, exciting, wondrous life we all know as earth ! Only God has this power. Buddha. Jehovah. Mohammed. Krishna. Whatever name you want to give Him. God does exist. Not above the clouds peering down at us but on our world. God is an ever opening flower, an ear listening to us. He speaks to us across the ages for eternity."

He looked at her in awe, her passion a fresh breath of life, "so why are we here ?" Jon asked.

She smiled, "Its all about faith. Learning what God is through our own experience, to seek the truth, to seek the balanced judgement, to seek one's very soul !"

She thought for a few moments, "I remember Switzerland, where I met my husband. I learnt there that the mountains hold the secret. They are immovable. Strong. Unyielding. Though the clouds sometimes cover their heads their peaks know the secret of the seasons. From these peaks on a clear day you can see forever !" She put a hand firmly on his shoulder, "perhaps God's majesty is the mountains." And turning to go she added, "good luck !"

Jon was silent as they headed north. Zetler had already announced an "impromptu stop" in a small east Lancashire village, "It seems, " he had said over the noise of the traffic and the radio, "we need some encouragement. We will have to steel ourselves against the danger." Zetler turned the music down so it was a mere background hum.

He spoke with a touching sensitivity revealing some of his childhood memories, "I remember as a boy in the face of great danger, at least it seemed that way as a boy, my father saying to me, 'son you have a choice, you can be true to yourself or true to others, you cannot be both. If you are true to others you will lie to yourself winning fair weather friends. You may have a fine career as you claw your way to the top agreeing with everyone but gradually a cancer will grow, that of cynicism !"

His gazed off down the road and continued, "you will be asked to seek the truth but only reveal it as long as agrees with everyone else's *truth*. One day you will wake up and realise it's all some awful twisted game in which you may have position or power but you will have lost yourself. Search for the truth. With this mission you will be able to look in a mirror with pride !' What we are being asked to do is no different. We must seek out truth with no compromises."

His hands gripped the wheel and he shuffled in his seat, "For us. Well. We must find that truth and believe it to the end...."

Some hours later they arrived in a quiet back street at an unassuming terrace house. Jon parked the car in the small drive and Zetler rang the door bell. They were greeted by a middle aged man smoking a pipe and carrying a mug of coffee in one hand.

"Come in," he said, "come in. You're all most welcome" and he ushered them inside apologising for his casual dress, an old holed green cardigan and threadbare slippers. He lead them through to the parlour, a small room, comfortable, cosy but rather dingy with curtains drawn and only a small table lamp illuminating the gloom.

Richard Murray had known of his powers for some years and he believed they were gifted to him at his mother's death when he was just a boy. His gift, as he preferred to call it, had been tried on many occasions, once in the well-publicised gaze of television when he had contacted the spirit of a missing child. That particular seance had lead to the discovery of the child's body and the eventual arrest of the murderer. The murderer subsequently confessed but committed suicide in his cell. Murray had gone on to speak to the murderer some days after the suicide on the same programme.

He had, in some ways, become blasé about his abilities and once described them as, "simply the gift to call the spirits as if by telephone."

Meanwhile, as with many genuine mediums, he had been labelled a fraud and a charlatan but had never been proven to be so by the scientists, as is so often the case when science can not explain events outside their knowledge.

As a child, he remembered watching a butterfly struggling to break free from the cocoon. Desperate to help he had taken a pin and gently eased apart the capsule to allow the butterfly from its silky prison. As it flew to a nearby branch he had noticed that the butterfly's wings were not red as the others nearby but were grey and colourless. He had explained his observations to his biology teacher. She told him how in its struggle the butterfly needed to send blood to its wings to ignite their patterns and colours.

Richard had therefore realised early in his life that creativity was gifts that only come with pain and struggle. He had therefore ignored his detractors focusing on his talent and using it for good wherever and whenever he could.

In the past Richard Murray had met many spirits. He had come to believe that they were not ghosts but simply voices from another plane - another time and space.

Richard made himself comfortable and soon drifted off into a trance. His breathing became slow and shallow. There was silence for some moments, then he spoke.

"Jon. It's me Daniel. Long time. No speak !" Jon recognised the voice immediately as his brother's. It's seemed to greet him in recognition. "You've done well ! You've travelled a long way but you're on the way home again !" Daniel greeted them and was congratulatory. "I've been chosen as the voice. There are many who are here waiting for you. Many who send their love. We know you can succeed. We know you will send them homeward."

The voice faded and returned and Daniel spoke with conviction and confidence. "The pieces of the puzzle are falling into place. The conjunction is almost upon us to bring rest to the restless, peace to the tormented and sleep to the ones who wait. Your task will be one of exorcism. It will carry you beyond all you know, all you'd ever imagined and all you'd ever dare to dream...dare to dream...dare to dream..."

The voice faded out and echoed in a whisper around the room and Richard began to take deeper breaths again. He woke and opened his eyes looking around the room to reorient himself. His face looked drained.

He managed to smile. "They came didn't they ?" He said with a thin smirk.

Chapter 18.

Angels in the Architecture

*"Many have walked into a room and felt themselves to have been there before,
watching as a scene unfolds, knowing exactly what is to happen as if in a waking
dream. It does not happen by command or by invocation. However, there are the seers,
who have the true power of foresight."*

Jarrat Toldon, Chronicles of the Future

*"And we can relax on both sides of the tracks,
And maniacs don't blow holes in bandsmen by remote control."*
Roger Waters

*T*hey cut across the border country in the late afternoon entering
Edinburgh from the South. Having stayed in modest hotels for most of
their journey Zetler decided he would treat them and they checked into
the luxurious Caledonia Hotel at the end of Princes Street. A short taxi
ride round the base of the castle took them into Old Town where they
wandered the cobbled streets and wynds of the Royal Mile. The air was crisp
and the town quieter than when Jon had visited at the height of the festival
some weeks before. The town had not quite been given back to the students
and the bars were busy but not crowded. They found a corner in the Jolly
Judge and Drew bought a round of drinks.

Relaxed as they were they talked of their journey, their home towns, their
experiences, their lives in fact anything except the future. They all believed
they were reaching the end of their quest with only a short drive to Jon's
home in Aberdeenshire. It was during that evening that they realised they
had become a team, each with their own particular strengths, each prepared
to help the other when the going got rough and stronger together than as one.

The conversation turned to Scotland and the Devolution Bill that had been
passed giving the Scots the right to govern their own futures and the first
steps to full Scottish independence. Many had suffered since the time of
Wallace, The Bruce, Culloden, Glencoe and the Highland Clearances. There
was a wind of change and it was change for the good, the time had come for
freedom from an uncaring greedy bureaucracy. New purple flowers grew on
the thistle.

Jon decided to return to the hotel and sat in the lounge deciding to practise the voyeuristic hobby of "people watching". His seat was a good vantage point to observe the customers and staff as they made their way through the reception area to the revolving doors. He had seen faces he recognised, politicians and businessmen, rich shoppers and couples up for a weekend. He wondered why they were there, what they were doing and if they had any idea of the ripple effect of their smallest actions. Through the revolving door came faces he recognised. It was Zetler and Annelise who returned from Old Town.

After Zetler bid Annelise goodnight he seated himself next to Jon. "Jon," he said, "we have come along way, you and I. We have seen many things and got to know each well. Now is the time to reveal a little more of the picture."

Jon put down his book, beckoned a waiter over and ordered two whiskeys. "Okay," Jon said clasping his hand together nervously, "I'm ready."

Zetler sat back, "Jon do you know much about your ancestors ?"

Jon thought and said, "Well, they came from Wales, settling in the Midlands around 1800. One side of the family emigrated to America and genealogists have traced another branch to France and Spain."

"Good," Zetler said, "but you have no knowledge back to around 1600 ?"

"No not at all." Jon said, "I imagine them to be Methodists, my fathers family originated from the Welsh borders."

"You're correct," Zetler said, "your ancestors were Welsh. They came from a small farming community in mid-Wales called Rhayader and they were religious zealots." He took a sip of the whisky that had arrived as they talked. "Your father, many generations ago, was a minister in the town. It was a cruel time and was a time of witch hunts and bigotry."

Jon was perplexed by Zetler's story but did not interrupt, "Josiah was responsible for burning a young woman at the stake for witchcraft. Her son, Ranulf, was only twelve years old and sought revenge on Josiah and his seed. Josiah, his wife and children, except one, were killed when their house was destroyed by fire some five years later, it was known that Ranulf had started the blaze but he escaped capture. Your descendent, Josiah's youngest son, survived as a mercenary serving under Sir William Blane."

"Surely that is long forgotten and over ? It was 400 years ago !" Jon said.

"You're right Jon. But, it is not over. The son survives through the power that he serves. Since his 30th birthday he has not aged and grows ever more powerful. And he seeks you Jon, his malice and vendetta live on."

Extract from the essay "Growth and Spread of Immorality"

Very Reverend Henry Peake
Bishop of York

Why does evil thrive ?

After the disaster of Culloden the highland population had been decimated by the harsh weather, famine, emigration and the red coats. The Scots died in ditches, on ships bound for the New World, in the wilderness of the new land, in the prison ships on the Thames, on the gallows at the roadside. The Gaelic language, the tartan and the bagpipes were destroyed and the Highlanders were a broken lost people.

One hundred years later in that same New World the native Indian was driven from their land in the same callous way by a new adventurous breed. Millions across the prairies in those tribes died in the same way from the bullet, the cold, the hunger. Of the millions that took to the trail of tears, leaving only the dead behind them, only a few thousand of their descendants survive.

Two hundred years later Adolf Hitler and his followers instigated the final solution, an action that devastated the Jewish community removing millions to death camps across Eastern Europe. Of the millions wrenched from their families, robbed of their possessions, crammed into cattle trucks, murdered in the gas chambers and burned to obliterate the crime, only a few thousand survived.

Those holocausts were murderous, bigoted, cruel, twisted, inhumane, harsh and callous. They had an evil nationalistic and fascist purpose, the destruction and annihilation of a race. The deliberate and premeditated cleansing of the history books. The purging of a blight, the expurgation of guilt, the obliteration of a civilisation that threatened.

The holocausts were instigated in the name of civilisation and future strength, in the name of power and progress.

The holocausts were the deaths of a nation but, the holocausts were the first sparks of the fires of new ideals and new nations.

Was it any wonder the songs of those people are sad, forlorn and bitter. It is any wonder those songs are full of hope ? Is it any wonder that the evil that initiated it lives on and still thrives ?

* * * * *

Ranulf held her in his arms and caressed her, feeling her warmth and becoming intoxicated by her perfume. He ran his fingers through her dark hair and nuzzled in her neck. He looked into her eyes as they entwined in passion and lust.

He thought of her beauty and of her deep dark blue eyes. He knew she had been unfaithful to him, not in any sexual way, but he knew she had begun to have a conscience and the riches that he gave her would no longer hold her.

They made love with the same passion of their first time and with an intensity born of two souls bound by experience. Their bodies sank into the sheets drained from their love making and he turned to her again and gliding his hand along her side and over her breasts and shoulders and on to her neck.

And as he looked into her dark eyes he realised that she had out lived her usefulness. Her conscience would eventually betray him. That was certain.

His hands felt the veins and muscles in her neck and gently placed his hands across her windpipe pressing with all his strength to crush the life from her.

Her eyes opened wide in stark terror but it was too late. Her arms and legs flailed for an escape but her struggles and cries were stifled by his strong torso.

She passed out. He released his grip to pull a clean, white starched pillow over her soft mouth and held it over her face until there was no pulse, no heartbeat and she was dead.

Then he showered and dressed and drank a large glass of vodka.

He packed a bag, from tonight he would not return to his lair.

He gazed at her beautiful face and ran his fingers over her cold and bluing flesh and he cried. He sobbed in sorrow, in anger, with a fear that grew like a tumour in his heart.

Revenge had been born and the evil had been released. An evil so unquenchable that like a drug it becomes an obsession and eventually an addiction.

From tonight the voices would be forever silent.

They would come to him no more.

Tonight, he had crossed the final line.

* * * * *

There was a knock on Drew's hotel room door and after pulling on some jeans and a T-shirt he answered it.

"Hi !" Said Annelise nervously as he opened the door a few inches, "it's me ! Can I come in ?"

"Sure," Drew said, surprised to see her, "Sorry about the mess. I've been watching a movie, it really wasn't worth it."

Annelise sat on the bed, "Drew , Zetler asked me to give you this." She took a package from her basket. It was gift wrapped in plain blue paper and tied with a white ribbon and a star shaped bow.

Frowning, Drew took it from her and carefully undid the wrapping paper. Anticipation thumped in his heart. Inside was a smaller parcel wrapped in brown paper and posted from a town in North Carolina. Drew removed this to reveal, wrapped in tissue, a small, flat, silver box with engraving on the lid. The hallmark was quite clear underneath and the lid bore two initials scrolled together - E. M.

"He said it belongs to you !" Annelise said.

Drew shrugged and opened the lid of the box. He held it in the palm of his hand. It felt familiar to him as if it was something he thought he had lost a long time ago that had been returned to him.

"Zetler said it was mine ?" Drew shrugged again but, something stirred inside him, something in his Celtic soul, sea spray and the crashing of the waves echoed in his heart.

Then, he remembered the family legend, told by his aunt and his father. Of his grandfather. How his grandfather, wife and daughters had emigrated to the States from Ireland taking passage on the Titanic, how his grandfather had been lost with the other souls while his grandmother and aunts had survived. How on their eventual arrival in America they had settled in New York and how his father Eric had been born nine months later.

The cigarette case had lain on the bed of the Atlantic seventy years until it had been found by Dr Ballard's expedition and later plundered some years after by the French voyages which set out to make money from the underwater graveyard.

It gave him a strange warm feeling to hold the box. Something that was once his grandfather's, whom he had never met, was returned to his family, a token of his grandparent's love. It gave him hope as great expressions of affection and love are bound so to do, "So, what goes around, comes around !" He exclaimed, holding it up to the light.

Universitaet des Wiens
Memo

From : Andreas Lilletage   To : Prof Josef Muller

Subject : Result of Analysis of Skeletal Remains

Further to our investigation to ascertain the identity of the remains found during our summer's extensive archaeological research within the burial vaults of the ruined palace of Hohenlange to the South of Vienna last month.

As you are aware, my colleagues and I have successfully identified the other six skeletons found within the vaults. Their position within the chamber, condition inside what little remained of the caskets and their features (after facial reconstruction) match portraits and recorded pictorial features of the Hohenlange family.

The seventh skeleton was, before today, a mystery. Unlike the others it was in a simple pine casket and bore no resemblance to the family line. It was wrapped in a form of sacking shroud used during the period for the burial of paupers. However the golden cord that secured the end was very unusual.

An examination of the bones and teeth confirm that the body is that of a young man aged approximately 35 years. We ascertained death to be between 1790 and 1794. As you are aware the palace was totally destroyed by fire and subsequently abandoned in Christmas of 1794.

The skeleton was in excellent order and the hands particularly well developed. The body had no jewellery or identifying features though the clothes were of a reasonable quality with the cuffs being particularly worn and threadbare.

The skull still had a small amount of hair available for analysis some of which has sent to Salzburg for testing by the Reichspolitizei. The bones and hair show evidence of arsenic and we are therefore convinced the man died of poisoning. Detectiv Hans Schroeder of the Salzburg police concurred with this cause of death. He then proceeded to compared the DNA of the strand of hair to that of a lock of hair held in a museum within the city.

Furthermore, the graphical facial reconstruction which computer technicians produced last week reveal a striking resemblance to portraits that I have in front of me at this time.

Sir. My colleagues and I are convinced that all the evidence points to the remains that we hold in our university vault being none other than those of composer Wolfgang Amadeus Mozart.

Chapter 19

Coming Home

*"As we walk through our lives we should realise what a wonder it is to be here !
Many will lament their existence not realising they have it within themselves to
change the lives they lead. Revel in your times ! There is so little of it."*

Jarrat Toldon, Chronicles of the Future

"I didn't know when I was lucky, discontented feeling bad,
Filled with envy for possessions, other people had.
With my family all around me, I've all the riches I can hold,
I'm a beggar, sitting on a beach of gold"

Mike Rutherford

*T*he next morning they were to leave the Caledonia straight after
breakfast and Zetler had moved the Espace to the front of the hotel
where it competed with the many taxis that drew up regularly
depositing visitors and shoppers outside. All their luggage had been
loaded and they waited to board but of Drew there was no sign. He had
handed his bags to Jon and dashed off in the direction of Charlotte Square.

"Do you know where he's gone ?" Asked Annelise.

"Not a clue," Jon shrugged his shoulders, "but he seemed to know where he
was going and he was in a big hurry !"

Fifteen minutes later he reappeared dodging the traffic of Princes Street with
a broad, perhaps even smug, smile on his face.

"Hah !" He said in exclamation as he loaded into the front seat, "they
wondered where I got it but they were pleased to see it anyhow !"

"What are you talking about ?" Annelise asked slightly frustrated with Drew
who was acting like a mischievous teenager hunched in the front seat.

"The chess piece ! I took it to where it belongs ! The National Museum hold
four sets of pieces. One of the sets was missing a king. I have corrected that !"

At the museum the piece was being examined in some awe. They spoke of
how the strange American benefactor had walked into the museum with it
wrapped in a table napkin and given it to one of the staff at the reception
desk, "Say ! I think this belongs to you !" He had said handing the lost
treasure to them.

Early in the afternoon they arrived at Jon's croft in the heart of Aberdeenshire, though croft was a poor description for what was quite a large property. It was, in fact, two stone buildings joined into one and further extended with two wings, one containing a workshop and the other a music room.

The house was spacious and rambling having five bedrooms and a large sitting room with a huge fire at the one end which Jon had already lit and which sent a warm glow around the house.

Behind the house was a large open paddock of about an acre with an orchard in one corner, the trees of which were heavy laden with ripe apples, pears and plums.

Across the gravel courtyard was the disused Smithy, an old, dusty, granite single story building with a great set of oak double doors that were locked with a rusty chain and padlock and which rattled in the wind.

They had parked in the courtyard and unloaded the luggage but, as they arrived Jon had noticed Zetler's eyes were immediately drawn towards the Smithy and he seemed to view it with some apprehension.

"The Gateway ?" Jon speculated but Zetler made no comment.

Jon allocated each of his guests a room and began arranging bedding and getting the boiler fired up to take away the stale chill of the house. Each had a room with a view over the garden and fields beyond down to the sea that could be seen on a clear day. This was quite rare, usually a haar misted the view for at least a mile in land. Zetler soon found his way around the cottage and set about brewing a large jug of coffee. The aroma of fresh coffee soon wafted around the house.

A little over an hour after they had arrived they were gathered around the kitchen table nursing mugs of Zetler's strong brew and nibbling shortbread.

"Well," said Zetler, raising up his mug up in a toast. "We have arrived, my children. Cheers and Good Health!" They all reciprocated his toast and he added, "Remember, over the next few days you should not be afraid. We have come to a very powerful place but each of you has a guardian !"

They knew what he said to be true.

"There are many ghosts here and soon we must face and free them," he continued, "you have travelled far and tomorrow is but a heart beat away."

Under the table Annelise reached over and squeezed Drew's hand in reassurance.

Jon craved solitude in his beloved Aberdeenshire countryside. With his Monza still in the multi-storey car park at Heathrow, he borrowed the Espace and adjusted the driving seat to make himself comfortable. He turned the key and it hummed contentedly into life. It was a beautiful September day. The leaves were beginning to fade to the gold of autumn browns and there was still warmth left in the early evening sun.

He opened the car's sun roof and let the cold fresh air replace the plastic stuffiness. He decided to drive the short distance to the cliff tops at Slains where he parked the car and put on his wind proof long-coat that covered him neck to toe almost touching the ground. As he approached the haunted ruins of Slains Castle, the wind seemed to swell in warning. He clutched the coat around him and turned his back to the wind.

At the edge of the cliff he stared down at the sea crashing on the craggy rocks far below him. He watched the ebb and flow of the waves as they beat against the black glistening granite and he noticed how his breath matched the powerful rhythm. As he took in a deep breath the sea seemed to withdraw. As he breathed out the sunlight glinted briefly on the wave crests and then broke in it's tempest on to the headland. He seemed to feel the heartbeat of the earth and could hear the music of the spheres.

Jon stood on the cliff top, hands deep in his pockets for warmth, gazing out to the clear horizon that merged with the crisp blue sky out toward Norway and the oil platforms with their small crews that warred and battled with the elements for energy and profit every day. The sea seemed so wild and tempestuous on such a calm sunny day but he knew the North Sea could be deceptively cruel.

He faced the expanse of an empty sea, watching as the sky started to glow with the oncoming sunset and a new night time of stars. The wind wrapped itself around him and enveloped him while the last beams of the sun behind him warmed his back. He closed his eyes and held his arms aloft in an act of submission to the elements. It seemed to strengthen him and he indulged in the sensations.

He took long deep breaths of cold sea air that refreshed and cooled him giving him life and energy. The wind whistled like a banshee round the ruins, buffeting his body and tearing at him, caressing, twisting around his body, curling and murmuring around the torso, whipping his dark hair around his face and flapping his coat like a blustering banner behind him. He imagined that he had wings and was free to soar into the gathering starlit sky.

The zephyrs greeted him as an old friend, gently testing his resistance, following the contours of his form and flowing around him like water. The wind howled, the sea roared, the sun warmed him and Jon played like a child in the wind.

Back at the croft Drew and Annelise somehow knew it would be their last night together and they caressed each other for strength knowing that alone they were weak but together they were a powerful force.

Drew took Annelise by the hand and they lay down on the bed wrapping themselves around each other, two bodies as one.

There were no words, no force, no resistance, each other knowing instinctively what to do and knowing in this world this would be the last time.

It was a beautiful September day. The leaves were beginning to fade to gold of autumn browns but there was still a little warmth left in the early evening sun.

They had left the window of the room ajar to let the fresh evening air and it gave them new energy.

They touched, explored, enjoyed each other's warmth, tenderness and love.

They felt themselves looking down on earth with a passion that crashed in on the rocks way below him. Love could be wild and tempestuous on such a day and they knew it could be deceptively cruel.

They kissed, soft lips, warm, gently and electric sending life running through their hearts like an elixir bringing each other back to life and glowing with a summer's sunshine.

They lay hand in hand, heart in heart for warmth, gazing into each other's eyes to the clear horizon of their souls and they drifted high above the mountain tops with the expanse of world spread before them, watching as the sky starting to glow with the oncoming sunset and a new night time of stars. They could feel the heartbeat of the earth and could hear the music of the spheres.

They wrapped themselves around each other enveloping themselves as the last beams of the day's sun warmed them. They closed their eyes and submitted to their passion that gave them strength.

Their love refreshed them giving each other life and energy and their passion sang like an angel, moving their bodies and massaging them, caressing, twisting around their bodies and whipping their hair around their faces.

They greeted new life as an old friend, following the contours of their bodies and flowing around each other like water. They felt themselves floating, flying, moving ever higher, ever skyward. Outside the wind howled, the sea roared and the sun warmed them and they played like children in the wind.

In the lounge below, Zetler sat in Jon's great oak carver chair warming his bones in front of the fire and nursing a glass of Glenfiddich, a half empty bottle of which he had found by the fire side.

He stared into the glowing embers and thought of the future, he knew they had almost reached their goal but the game was not yet over.

Tomorrow, he knew, there was a cross-roads in space and time, three dimensions intersecting this time, this world, the next world. Roads that ran almost parallel which met only to part again.

He knew they would only have one chance, he knew there would be sacrifices. He could already feel Ranulf and his evil close at hand. Perhaps he was watching, observing even now.

If they were successful the equilibrium that had been broken would finally be restored. If they were successful, those in the wait state would be freed to return again and Ranulf's gateway would be closed forever.

The chess piece had been returned to its brothers, the cigarette box and prayer book were back with there ancestral owners. All were now back in their rightful homes with only the sword remaining. He knew that the return of the objects had already set events in motion that would open doors and reveal some of the secrets that had been hidden.

Zetler had already read in this morning's newspaper of the discovery and identification of Mozart's body in Vienna. He smiled in satisfaction, if they failed, his efforts and those of his group, had not been completely in vain.

He had learned long since, how long he could not remember, how seemingly insignificant actions could cause something of much greater consequence to occur.

The world was held in syncronicity. Disruption created ripples that sometimes caused catastrophe or apocalypse. He and future generations would be on guard for such events.

If they were successful he knew his work would continue and his journey would go on as it would for all. That was the way of things. He would always find himself moving onward, rarely resting, seeking the final goal, a quest that he knew he would achieve one day.

Now, he was content to rest. To drink in the warm crackle of the fire and the aqua vitae of the whisky. To rest, opening his heart to peace. Soon he slept.

* * * * *

The black Range Rover rolled, engine off, crunching across the gravel. The vehicle dimmed its lights and parked, silent in the gateway. The night was black as tar and the sky was dotted with stars, the Milky Way crystal clear with billions upon billions of twinkling lights.

Ranulf took out a small hip flask from his inside jacket pocket and took a long swig of its contents. He felt the warmth of the alcohol course like hot nectar through his veins. He pressed the button of the electric window and opened it to sniff the air like a hound. He could smell the wood smoke of the fire drifting over the fields and could see the lights of the house.

From the distance he could discern an old man seated in front of the fire, the face illuminated in the orange glow of the coals. It was him !

He knew he was close. He knew they were close. He smiled with satisfaction. They do not have long !

"If only they knew who the hell they were fighting", he cursed them for their stupidity.

He cursed them as he had cursed that woman as she had choked between his hands. So beautiful, cruel and bitter. At the end she had had no respect for him and he had certainly cared little for her.

"Treacherous bitch," he spitted and rung the stiffness out of his hands as if he could still feel her throat between them.

Her death had given him that extra strength, the edge, the power to defeat and conquer again.

He felt invincible, powerful and destructive. No prisoners would be taken. No quarter given. No mercy.

He knew exactly what their plan was, it had been tried before and without success. He had been run close that time but they didn't realise his strength was in their own naive goodness.

He felt, as he had felt it before, that the time was approaching. A pull that he could not escape, dragging him closer and closer to the edge. Tomorrow he would meet at the time cross-road.

But, he'd played the role and the scene before. He knew his entrances, he knew his cues, he knew his entrance and his exits and he knew his final lines. He would need no prompt to complete the act.

Besides, the nagging voices in his head had been strangely silent.

Chapter 20

Arrival

"It is sad how many lives and how much time is wasted on the mundane. We are gifted with a powerful force of life and not to use it to its fullest potential is a crime ! There are few who strive to reach the heights and even fewer who will reach the pinnacles !"

Jarrat Toldon, Chronicles of the Future

"More than just survival, more than just a flash,
More than just a dotted line, more than just a dash !
More than high performance, more than just a spark
More than just a bottom line or a lucky shot in the dark !"

Neil Peart

As day turns into darkness, as sure as the cosmos, each night millions of souls enter the dream state. Conjuring images from the sub-conscious, over which they have no control and which reveal, sometimes with clarity and sometimes ambiguity, inner hopes and fears. We awake with only a few images from those dreams, snatches of a taste or a feeling, most are forgotten in the haste, harshness and cold reality of the morning.

There are few lucky ones who can control and remember their dreams and they derive strength and comfort from them. In our story, there is one who never dreams. His mind, in sleep, is a black void in which no images enter and from which no new ideas form, a barren wasteland in which no thought will seed and grow. Since the beginning of his evil days he had shunned the light and sought the darkness.

Hiding deep in his soul there was a spark of redemption, a tiny glimmer of regret that had smouldered and gnawed at his conscience for over four centuries. He had fought to bury it but like a green shoot fights for the sunlight it would surface. After half a millennium the world had turned many times on its journey through the heavens. Many lives had been lost in the futile wars we had fought. The earth had turned in its orbit too slowly for Ranulf but his life had finally come full circle, a leech-like power that was once at its zenith was beginning its decent.

We must be on our guard. As experience and history teach us, victory, even in the face of apparent certainty, is never assured.

* * * * *

It was still pitch black as Zetler dressed. Wrapping himself in his coat he walked across the courtyard to the Smithy. There was something he wanted to confirm and he knew at this hour, the moment between night and day, the spirits would be resting and at their weakest. The door was wide open, wedged with two granite bricks and he entered without hesitation or hindrance. The building felt cold but not chilly, dark but not evil; it felt benign. He decided that his course of action should be bold.

Standing in the gloom he called out. "Are you awake ?"

He was answered with silence, just a breeze from the doorway and the trees rustling in the lane. He called again, commanding and this time much louder. "Do you sleep ?"

Again silence, but, then, maybe a stirring. He walked over to the well and taking the large heavy torch he carried he illuminated the mossy depths. The brick sides of the well were bright forest green with vegetation and shadows seemed to skim the surface of the water and dance under the beams of light.

But, there was a presence, he could feel it. There was something that told him this building also had a soul. It was indeed a powerful place and he hoped it was a benign spirit. He turned and looked down feeling a distant rumble vibrating the ground beneath his feet. At the doorway something glowed and grew, a manifestation of some type. Within a moment it had become substantial. It was a tall, bearded middle-aged man, his hair long and curled. In his hand he held a small iron mallet and he wore a long leather apron. Zetler recognised the apparel of a blacksmith.

"Are you come for them ?" The voice said.

"Yes !" Zetler said, "we are come. They will be freed this day !" Zetler promised.

"Good." The man said, satisfied and nodding his head in approval, "they have all paid a terrible price thus far." He thought a moment and then asked, "will you close up the gateway for good. It would be better for the future."

Zetler smiled, "Yes ! That will also be done !"

"Good." The man replied smiling, "that's good...."

With this his shape began to fade until his body was insubstantial and transparent. And he was gone.

Finally, all that Zetler could hear was the wind blowing the dry sycamore leaves that dance and whirl in celebration around the doorway.

It was early but Jon's mind was wide awake and alert. He opened the curtains and caught the first orange rays of a dawn glowing in the East which gently warmed his face. If this was to be his last day, it had a glorious beginning !

He walked over to the dressing table and picked up the notepad he had carried with him for some years as a diary and in which had documented his journey.

He opened it to the front page on which was written one of the first poem's he had ever written and he smiled as he thought about his wife and their love.

Floundering

Where is your heart when I look in you eyes, Where is the love you give me
Where is the spark, the static of life, Is it sunk and presumed lost at sea

Where is the ship that brings me surprise, Where is the cargo you keep me
Where is the sail of the cutter of love, Is it sunk and presumed lost at sea

We are lost in the doldrums, Sailing loves oceans, Riding the storms of the sea,
We are battered and broken, Sailing loves oceans, but, you're sailing back home to me

We are cutting it close to the storm of tomorrow, We are pushing the edge of our days
We are battered and broken cast on the rocks, No beacon to brighten our ways

Bring me a lifeboat to save our survivors, Take me to some close safe haven
Harbour my love in blue calming waters, Let me lie at the quay side till dawn.

Those early days had been hard, but in the face of adversity they had had strength. He remembered how they had met, the tiny flat they had in Birmingham and the frugal way they lived in those days.

Life had seemed so simple. Food, warmth and a roof over their heads but through the years it had become so complicated.

He felt a twinge of sadness and sat down at the window to wait for the dawn to grow into a new day.

Meanwhile, across the misty, haar covered fields, parked in a gateway the black Range Rover's windows were streaming with rivers of condensation. The autumn night had been cold and damp and a light frost had formed like a dust of sugar icing on the windows and roof.

Ranulf's night, wrapped and curled in a blanket on the back seat, had been an uncomfortable, restless and sleepless one and though he had not dreamed, he had been wakened through the night by images that flashed before him from his twisted, dark and blighted past.

Images of the wars he had seen, of the destruction he had been part of and the lives he had destroyed. With those dreadful images were the pitiful faces of his victims.

Their lives stained his soul with their blood and he was suddenly struck by the futility of it all. He had never been to blame though. At least that's what he thought. He had always been pushed on; no,driven on, by those voices. Do this. Do that. Do as you are told. Obey. How could he ever do otherwise ? They would have destroyed him without a doubt had he even thought to refuse !

They had tormented him for years and he longed to be free of them. He realised that there was only one way and that route, that path, he dreaded with all his heart. He had finally concluded that perhaps immortality had its disadvantages.

His memory had not faded with time and he was constantly reminded of the past. Though he had had many victories there were also many failures, bad times he wished to forget.

Those images had been so vivid that it was difficult to clear them from his mind. Spirits, ghosts, ghouls and souls drifted before him, the dreams of times past. But, they did not frighten him; he only feared oblivion.

Perhaps reincarnation, returning many times was not as bad ? But as whom ? With whom ? Living where ? In what ? Living as what ? And how ?

He really did not think he could bear poverty. Or hardship. Cold. Or hunger.

He plumped up the pillow he had made of his jacket and turned over, wrapping the blanket tightly around him. He closed his eyes blocking out the dawn and hoped to get just a few more hours sleep, he would need them if he were to be victorious that next day.

That night the voices in his head had not come to comfort him and Ranulf now slept restlessly.

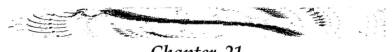

Chapter 21

Crossing the Bridge

"There can be little worse than being trapped in a time in which you have no desire to be. To be humiliated by showing respect to those for whom you have none, bending like a reed in the wind when every sense urges you to howl like a storm. Let no man be an unjust jailer, let no man clip another's wings !"

Jarrat Toldon - Chronicles of the Future

"Everybody lives and loves and laughs and cries
and eats and sleeps and grows and dies.
Everybody in the whole of the world...."

Steve Hogarth

*T*he morning dawned with brightness and colour as red, hazy beams of light penetrated the cold mists of daybreak and turned the sky across the horizon a deep coral. The bitter chill of the night was replaced by the bright warmth of another new day that penetrated every hollow and evaporated the insubstantial mist. The earth turned, the sun shone across the land, the waves crashed unrelentlessly on the shores and the wind sent the clouds scudding across the sky on a seemingly eternal quest.

Today would be one when mankind would live, mankind would die, mankind would love and mankind would cry.

Would it be a day when mankind returned to and recognised the simple pleasures of food, shelter, love and health ?

For most, it would start as an ordinary day but would be remembered for all time across all the planes and dimensions for its extraordinary events. A long day when some souls would be freed and others fettered.

Would it be a day when sorrow outweighed joy ? Would it be a day of sadness or celebration ? Would there be a reason or a purpose ?

One could only be sure that no matter how the dice fell, that whoever won the day, the balance between sorrow and joy that rules the cosmos, would be eventually be in equilibrium.

* * * * *

Zetler had called a meeting late in the afternoon and they all gathered around the warm glow of the wood fire with coffees or something stronger; Drew with a Jack Daniel's and Zetler with an Ansbacher brandy.

"Well, my friends, we have travelled far and I hope we have learnt many things. Today sees the end of our journey." Zetler said as an introduction.

"It is our aim to destroy the being we know as Ranulf. We must trap him by deception and present him for trial where he can answer for his many crimes. Our bait, cruel word but apt in the circumstances, will be Jon, who in all of this is the closest to Ranulf and more likely to succeed in luring him. We will use Annelise, who's connection with Reinhardt who is also trapped will act as a beacon and help to lead the ones waiting away. I am sure their liberation will weaken Ranulf."

"Jon, meanwhile, will be used to lead Ranulf to the next plane where a trial of some type, I am unsure of the details in these circumstances, can be arranged. It is Jon's presence and his connection to Ranulf's tragedy that I am hoping will make Ranulf follow too closely. It is only outside the first and second worlds and outside the Wait State that he can be destroyed."

"So, how do you get Annelise and Jon there ?" Drew asked.

"Unfortunately there is but one way to send them on that journey." Zetler replied ominously.

"And what do I do ?" Drew added.

"You are the voice in this world. You will help me to call them back." Zetler looked seriously at Drew, "If we are unsuccessful they will not return." and the others shuddered as the implications dawned on them.

Zetler thought for a while and said, "Jon will have to face Ranulf. I have arranged for him to take the sword with him. It will be his only weapon and it is the final piece that can be used against Ranulf. We must make use of the strength we have gained during our travels. We must concentrate our minds on the task at hand. Today we must say our good-byes for, what ever happens, we must part." He said this with great sadness.

"Today sees a great conjunction when an equilibrium is to return, an extra moment to bring rest to the restless, peace to the tormented, sleep to the ones who wait, " and with this he raised his glass in a toast.

"Journey far and journey hopefully, my children !"

* * * * *

In the next plane the events that were unfolding were being watched with great interest.

In the place where justice and law had been born a meeting of the guardians had been called. Also in attendance in the great white room was any spirit who had an interest in the affair. The meeting was hushed as their elder guardian spoke.

During the short opening proceedings many questions concerning relatives, friends and loved ones had been raised and answered with patience by Carroll.

"Friends !" Carroll said, speaking from the floor at the centre of the forum, "It has taken us some time but the hour is now close."

Carroll was one of the most revered of all the guardians. He had been given great power and had used it with fairness and wisdom. He had begun his great journey many millennia before and reached the pinnacle of his soul to become one of only two eternal champions.

The other and the first, Jarrat Toldon, sat at his side listening with interest to the proceedings, occasionally writing his thoughts in a dark blue leather book he carried with him.

Carroll continued, "we must remind ourselves of the parts our parents play in our futures, how their actions cause events which their children will be forced to correct. Ranulf's evil had been caused by the evil of others," and he bowed his head in regret.

"We must thank Daniel for his time and effort. His delay has allowed us to resolve many issues and, if successful, will free many souls. Once these issues are resolved they allow the return of many time pieces which will complete the puzzle created by the past. Their return will healed the cracks we have seen. Across the four planes chaos has stained the fabric of time and could cause the seed of evil to root in many more. The matter must be resolved !"

Then, looking at Jarrat he said, "With faith, during this coming day we should see the end of that evil and the redemption of a soul." He clutched his hands together tightly and then in pleading said, "I ask you to pray for us and the courageous ones who, after all, are to make one of the ultimate sacrifices."

Carroll clutched his hands tighter, "Let them not be afraid. Let them be heroes !"

* * * * *

147

It is the nature of heroes that they do not realise they do anything heroic ! Their deeds are often undertaken on the spur of the moment and instinct rather than premeditation.

Placed in certain situations they reach out with their feelings and with an action turn the tide to snatch victory from defeat. At the end, when heroes fall they are trapped in corners with no hope of escape and no other options left, living only to die. Their lives are celebrated in a blaze of glory.

Through time there have been many such heroes and our story has introduced you to only a few.

Edgar; prepared to pay any price to free his friends and his beliefs from the burden of tyranny.

Christopher Colon; driven on by obsession, who opened up new thoughts and refused to be defeated by closed minds.

Don Orgaz; defending his land, life, loves and family from oppression, slavery and bigotry.

Mozart; working the last drops from his genius to create music and magic to the very end.

Eric Matheson; giving all for the love of his wife and children without hesitation or second thought.

Each and all fighting for what they believed and never thinking to count what was ultimately the highest cost.

It is the nature of villains that they are none of these things. They know nothing of sacrifice, believing truth to be some moving target and seeing traitors and treason as only a matter of dates. They are wrong !

And as the earth travels through time at 1000 miles an hour and the universe expands toward oblivion unknown and reluctant heroes are born and die teaching us lessons worthy of saga and legend.

And as the earth spins through the void it creates conjunctions, lines through the stars. Conjunctions that set off the first domino in the line or fit the final piece in some bizarre holistic and cosmic jigsaw in time and space. Conjunctions that span the dimensions and which are the beginning and the end of songs.

This day is such a conjunction.

* * * * *

Salzburg, Austria

In the grand cathedral Dom of Salzburg the Salzburger Mozarteum Orchestra premiered Mozart's completed "Requiem" that now included the newly found Glorianna. At its conclusion the whole audience rose in ovation stunned by the music's power, glory and beauty.

Two months later on Mozart's birthday his body was buried at a state funeral with full honours and was laid to rest in a specially commissioned mausoleum in Vienna's St Stephen's Cathedral. Mozart's birthday is henceforth declared an annual European public holiday dedicated to the promotion of arts and music.

Edinburgh, Scotland

In Edinburgh at the National Museum of Antiquities a special exhibition opens displaying some of the glories of Scottish culture and history. It includes a display of all five sets of the so-called Lewis Chess sets, three sets having been returned by the British Museum. The exhibition echoes a time of great national awakening and exceeds all capacity records.

Twelve months later the Scottish Independence Party wins 80% of Scottish seats in the British General Election and in a pact with the Socialist Democratic Party wins the airing of the Scottish Bill of Independence, the so-called "Bill of Dis-unity". The bill is passed.

Washington DC, USA

In Washington DC's Arlington Cemetery at 11:45 am, visitors describe the eternal flame, that burns over the stark black slate gravestone of President John F Kennedy, as flaring up for a few minutes. One witness said, "it seemed to burn brighter like a beacon that finally illuminates the truth !"

Atlantic Ocean

In the mid Atlantic during a freak storm a new floating exhibition displaying the artefacts recovered from the White Star liner SS Titanic sinks on its maiden voyage to New York. All 25 hands on board are saved due to the provision of unsinkable lifeboats. The vessel was utterly destroyed by the storm and all the artefacts on board the vessel are lost, returned by nature to the bed of the Atlantic. The last known position of the vessel is reported to be 41 degrees 46 minutes North 50 degrees 14 minutes West. The only surviving piece raised from the original wreck is an engraved silver cigarette case. Privately owned, it is gifted by an unknown benefactor to the National Museum of Ireland. It originally belonged to an Irish doctor who was emigrating to the States.

* * * * *

The world is full of "what ifs" and our lives are built and lived by them.

We can imagine a few. What if I lose my job ? What if I marry this person ? What if I had children ? What if.....and so on....

Let me pose a few to you the reader.

What if the John Fitzgerald Kennedy had not been murdered on that November morning ?

What if the Titanic had avoided the iceberg and sailed in to New York harbour passing the Statue of Liberty ?

Just imagine.

The consequences are too numerous to mention, so many they could echo through time for many millennia, so many they could ripple through the dimensions as a pebble cast into a pool and returning a million fold.

* * * * *

As arranged, at six they all met in the hallway of the croft.

They had each brought a blanket and Jon had also decided to bring a hip flask as protection against the chill of the Smithy. The air was not cold but the heat from the sun had long since gone and it seemed the night was already dressing in a dusky, blue cloak.

The hour struck six on the Grandfather clock in the croft's hall and the team walked from the front door, Zetler leading the way.

The gravel in the courtyard crunched under their feet and for the first time Jon noticed it's many hues and colours. The ground was a mosaic of pinks, greys, reds, blues and the sunset that was forming over toward the hill of Bennachie brightened and coloured them.

They walked slowly up the steps at the side of the Smithy. Drew turned to look at Annelise, her blonde hair reddened and darkened by the coral light and Annelise smiled broadly back at him. They entered the building and stood just inside its threshold. After a moments thought Zetler indicated they should place the blankets on the floor and kneel down on them.

And for the first time since they had met, as one, they prayed.

Chapter 22

Immortal. For a Limited Time

"There are many examples of lives sacrificed for motives which can not be justified. We have learnt that death in war is a hollow sacrifice but what of heroes giving life for redemption ? Their faith was unshakeable and they were rewarded beyond their imaginings !"

Jarrat Toldon, Chronicles of the Future

"We're only immortal . For a limited time..."

Neil Peart

nnelise and Jon lay on the cold stone floor of the Smithy, with a slight breeze blowing through the door, sending motes of dust dancing and spiralling into the air. Zetler and Drew knelt down beside them, Drew took Annelise's hand and Zetler put a hand on Jon's shoulder.

"If you are to return you must think of us," Zetler said, "we will both be here to call you back."

Drew squeezed Annelise's hand tightly, "If you don't come back I'm going to miss you," he said smiling, she returning it.

"To the next time," she said and then added, "will I dream ?"

"Yes ! Everyone dreams," Zetler replied comforting her. Then he asked "Are you both ready ?"

Jon reached into his jacket and pulled out a hip flask, "drink to us if anything happens," and then looking at Drew, "it's better than Jack Daniel's."

"Right !" Zetler said purposefully, "let's get on," and looking through the door at the fading glow of sunlight he said, "It seems a good day to die..."

Zetler reached over to the leather satchel and took out two small vials of beige liquid, a concentrate of cocaine and morphine saying, "You will drift into a deep sleep. The longer you sleep the more likely you are to stay on the other side. Remember your missions." He handed one bottle to Drew for Annelise and removed the stopper of the other. Jon and Annelise looked at each other then at Drew and Zetler and drank down the liquid.

And the rest was silence...

And Annelise slept, in her dream she could see Reinhardt in front of her, holding her, kissing her. She felt so tired, so heavy, so radiant. She felt calm and at peace. Her heart was warm and she glowed with love and happiness.

Annelise's visions began to fade. Her breath became shallow and her heart beat slowed to a falter and stopped.

And through her dream, images of the past were swept before her, of her father, mother, boyfriends, Drew, Reinhardt, her work, her failures, her achievements.

Then images of angels and demons, of love and hate, of goodness and evil. Then images of many past lives flashed before her like a slide show. Images of life and death, of birth and rebirth, of sleep and constant awakening.

She could feel her body travelling backwards being pulled upwards. Below she could make out her own body inert on the floor.

Her spirit self rose higher, through the roof of the Smithy and into the stars gathering in the clear night sky.

Lying next to her Jon slept, a deep slumber in which he could see his wife's face in front of him, holding him, kissing him. He felt so tired, so heavy, then so light. Jon's memory began to fade, his breath shallowed and his heart beat slowed and then stopped.

And through his dream. He dreamt of angels and devils, of love and hate, of goodness and evil. He could feel his body travelling backwards being pulled upwards and below he could see his body inert on the floor.

He viewed his life in microcosm. His journey over the past month, his life spread out before him like a tapestry. He felt as if it was being watched by not only himself but others. Analysing, scrutinising, perhaps even judging.

He saw his work, his friends, his family, his job, his failures, his weaknesses, his achievements, his home, his possessions, his anger, his happiness, his lies, his hopes, his dreams, his tears, his loves, his losses, his soul.

But most of all he thought of his wife, her perfume, her warmth and how he missed her and he thought he felt a tear rolling down his cheek.

Then a voice, reassuring and calming just as sadness began to creep upon him, "Rest, don't be afraid, we are here, don't be sad, don't be frightened" and he realised that it was his brother's voice. And he was at peace.

Annelise drifted without fear or worries, as she travelled the ultimate journey her heart was light and excited. She knew somewhere Reinhardt waited for her. She spun and twisted like a feather on a summer breeze tossed and blown wherever the breezes in this wind of time might carry her.

In her heart she could feel Reinhardt's love and passion but she also remembered her friend's final words of farewell. Drew's loving words, Jon's courage, Zetler's advice all echoed in her head like whispers from another existence. She thought of home, her mother, her father and for a moment wanted to return but her spirit knew her destiny and future lay elsewhere.

Her soul was full of purpose. She must be successful, she must find the gateway, she must find a way through, she must rescue the lost ones !

In the distance the speck of light towards which she drifted grew larger, shining like a bright morning star but with the intensity and harshness of a car headlight. It was a light that she had no desire to turn away from, a beacon in the darkness.

Instinctively she slowly put her arms out in an act of greeting and in the brilliance of the light she could see movement, a shadow, a figure. The figure's greeting was not cold but matter of fact, bright and crystal clear as ice and as she had been told. It was not a voice to be feared. The figure stepped forward and greeted her with a hug with filled her body with love and warmth.

"Annelise." The voice said, "Welcome home. I am your guardian. You have journeyed far but still have some way to go." The voice of her spirit guide was that of a woman, the face was wise and loving, maternal. "We must wait here just a few moments and then you may go on." Her guide said.

Annelise realised her body was now substantial. She was now dressed in a white flowing robe of silk, clinging to her and flowing like water around her slim body. They took a few paces and then her guide said, "beyond the gateway is another future. If you accept it only love can bring you back. Beyond it there is great danger and I cannot help you. Beyond it are many lost souls. I hope you can free them."

Ahead of her at the end of a tunnel of brilliant white light was an ordinary white door. She ran her fingers gently along its face feeling the contours and the grain of what she believed was wood. The door felt cold as marble and hard as stone. It felt strong but friendly.

It was a door to eternity and to the end of all songs. She turned the golden handle and with courage and hope in her heart she stepped through the portal.

17th April 1912

New York

It was early in the morning yet the docks were lined with thousands to greet the new pride of the White Star line. The journey has been uneventful, except for the near miss of an iceberg, which, three days previously, they had avoided.

The passengers were in party spirit and all were excited to arrive at their destination as Captain Smith eased the liner gently into New York harbour. The crowds waved frantically and visitors on Liberty Island waved flags and banners.

From the third class decks Eric Matheson and his family saw the tall buildings of New York for the first time. This was to be their new land and home and Eric felt it was not the end of a long journey but the beginning of another.

Some days later they had passed through the immigration processing on Ellis Island and travelled over land to Chicago. There Eric was meeting up with his elder brother and would share a thriving city doctor's practice.

The following year Eric and Kathleen had a son conceived in Ireland which they christened Eric. Two years later twin sons Michael and Martin were born. Michael and Martin followed their father's calling and became doctors joining a practice with their father and uncle.

The practice flourished. Encouraged by their father the sons branched out to specialise in viral and genetic studies. In the early sixties Martin and Michael Matheson discovered and isolated the gene that, when activated, caused a new disease known as AIDS.

Further research pointed the direction, just prior to their retirement, of the active genes that caused bone, breast and prostate cancers for which they received joint Nobel Prizes for Medicine.

It was Eric and Kathleen's proudest moment in long lives.

For mankind it was a moment of respite against the unrelenting enemy of disease.

For ripples in time it was just one of the many consequences of the Titanic sailing into New York on that cold April morning.

* * * * *

Jon began to feel heavier and insubstantial unable to feel his feet on the ground. He opened his eyes and was standing outside the oak doors of the Smithy or a representation of them, they didn't look wholly real.

Jon placed his hands on either door and pushed them open , it seemed to take tremendous effort and he strained to force them apart. Finally they gave way and swung open and he was bathed in a blistering bright white light that burnt his eyes. He put his hand to his face to shade his sight .

"Don't be afraid, " the voice said, "all is, as it ever is."

Gradually he put down his hand and became accustomed to the light. The Smithy was now a vast room, palatial in size and lined at either side with people viewing him with calm and concern .

"It is unusual for you to be allowed into our world," the voice explained, "but necessary, indeed unavoidable. My name is Carroll," the voice said, "I am a guardian."

Jon looked around the vast room. He gazed across the seas of faces and found his brother's. Daniel smiled and nodded in recognition and Jon moved to greet him. Carroll interceded.

Gently he led Jon away, "it may be possible to talk later with your brother depending on the outcome but we must begin the task. Please be seated."

Carroll pointed toward a large carver chair in the middle of the hall, his own fire side chair, "we were told you would be most comfortable in such a seat," Carroll said.

Jon nodded and took his place in the chair. He looked around the room and was able to recognise some of the faces. There were faces from the past, many long forgotten and a wave of guilt swept over him. How could he have forgotten so many ?

Jon sat back making himself comfortable and said, "I understand there is to be a trial."

"Yes, and the prisoner, Ranulf, will arrive soon. We must hope this is resolved swiftly. Many including your brother have waited here too long, there is now little time," Carroll said.

With this there was a rumble that reverberated like thunder. Jon could discern movement outside the open gateway.

Ranulf had finally arrived.

In the Smithy Drew and Zetler watched through the open door as outside the dusk was gathering and the first bright pinpoints of stars of the night sky twinkled into life. A breath blew back the door threatening to slam it.

Drew leapt up from where he crouched over Annelise's body and gently closed the door, barring it with the iron bolt.

As he closed the door he heard the voice in his head, "well done Drew ! Danger is close and that will slow it's pace." The voice was of Jarrat again.

It surprised him and he returned to his position next to Annelise like a faithful hound guarding his mistress.

"You have come far Drew. Your actions have put to rest one of our reincarnations. The truth shall always find itself."

The voice drifted and faded. Strong and then weak like a signal on a badly tuned radio.

"Have courage Drew," the voice said, "remember, we're only immortal for a limited time !" And it was again silent.

At the threshold of the door Ranulf had waited to recite his creed. He raised his arms to the heavens and the sky darkened.

"I am here my dark Lord !" He shouted, pleading, "give me your strength in this my hour ! Take me through the gateway."

Suddenly his body was convulsed and was racked by a force as terrifying and as brutal as death. He gritted his teeth in pain, " Y..e..s..s......n..o..w...!!!!" And he began to fade into the ice cold as the pain pierced his soul like a steel spike through his torso.

His body was surrounded with static and power flowed through him giving him strength. He sensed himself rising and travelling with a forward motion that sent him toward the source of the harsh bright light that surrounded him.

Then he felt the familiar force that struck him simultaneously on his back and stomach winding him and pushing him unceremoniously to the ground.

He took a breath and put his hands out to get up from the floor. He opened his eyes. He had arrived outside the gateway. He walked over to the door and pushed it until it bowed effortlessly and burst open wide blinding him with the bright light of the wait state.

But something seemed different.

Chapter 23

The Final Battle

"As children there were no limits to our imaginations. As adults, when faced with the insurmountable, we learnt how it is only fear that limits success. Without fear an impossible victory over an invincible adversary becomes conceivable."

Jarrat Toldon, Chronicles of the Future

"I want to go back to find, the innocent days that I left behind
I still believe they're holding ground, behind the battle lines
If it takes a million miles over land and sea
Going to swim through the rivers of purity
I know they still run free, behind the battle lines"

John Wetton

*I*n the chair, Jon felt his body lift and drift starward. With the sword at his side he concentrated on victory with Ranulf. As his spirit rose he could see the earth becoming a distant speck and the stars consumed by the darkness. As he rose he became cold and was hit with a blast of chill air that enveloped him like death.

And then a blinding white out !

He searched his soul and only views of the past remained. There was no future. He looked ahead, turn about and no future. Infinity. Eternity. Blank. Black. Immeasurable. Void. Nothing. If death had a form then this was it.

He felt as if his face and body were freezing. Ahead of him he could see the shape of a giant oak portal, the gateway. His thoughts drifted to his wife, his friends, Annelise, Drew. He concentrated again on victory over Ranulf, he must win, he must overcome - for the sake of the lost ones.

There was a sudden burst of golden bright light that forced apart the gate and allowed him to slip into the chamber. Then there was darkness and a bitter voice.

"Ah ! You've arrived ! It is you !" The voice said. It was a voice of evil. A voice of hatred. It was a voice from the shadows.

* * * * *

Zetler woke from his thoughts with a start and turned to Drew who was slumped against the Smithy wall, "It is time ! We must call them and we must call now !"

Hurriedly they walked across the Smithy where Jon and Annelise's bodies lay and they called, "Jon. Come back to your home ! Annelise ! Return to the one you love !" Zetler called and Drew repeated it. The reply was silence.

"Jon ! Come home ! Annelise ! Hurry home !" Drew called desperately.

Silence, except for the cry of a distant wind whispering through the eaves. Drew turned and sat with his back against the cold granite walls and looked over to Zetler who appeared to be praying over the lifeless forms of Annelise and Jon.

* * * * *

Annelise opened her eyes to the darkness of a large hall. Gradually her eyes became accustomed to the dark and faces whispered to her through the murk. In her heart she could feel a voice inside willing her to turn and walk back through the gateway.

"Who are you ? What do you want ? Come to take us home ?" The voices asked.

Annelise reached into her pocket and took out the cigarette case and held it above her head.

She called, "...Eric !" She called, "...Eric !"

Somehow the light in the room began to brighten and she could see hundreds of glinting sad eyes. The voices looked at each other in wonder.

"Does she want us ? Come to claim us ? What does she want ? Oh don't stay you mustn't stay !" And there was fear and weariness in their voices.

She reached again into her pocket and took out the prayer book and laid it on the ground.

She called, "...Njal ! Eric ? Orgaz ! Reinhardt ?" She called.

* * * * *

The Legacy of John Fitzgerald Kennedy

In 1963 JFK survived a bungled assassination attempt, after which a number of leading US defence officials and the Vice President were indicted. JFK was then elected US President for a second term.

His major policy decision of the term was to channel funds from the conflict in South East Asia to NASA and provide resources to win the race into space. By doing so the President successfully focused a nation's energies onto one achievable goal. During the mid sixties the South East Asian conflict ended as socialists won democratic elections in Vietnam, Cambodia and Laos.

Meanwhile in the space race the decision to increase spending was vindicated in July 1965 when the US's Apollo 3 landed on the moon and Astronaut James Lovell became the first human to walk on another world.

Early in 1968 JFK won a third term in office during which time various non-aggression pacts were signed with USSR and China. Late in 1968 the new space shuttle was used to transport humans to an orbiting space station that was used for staging further explorations of the lunar surface and as the first base for trips to Mars.

JFK meanwhile secures land for aggrieved Palestinians and an Arab/Israeli conflict is averted. He was awarded the Nobel Peace Prize the same year.

During the summer of 1971 a simulated Martian landing was executed by a joint US/USSR mission leading to the manned landing in the Spring of 1972 when Neil Armstrong became the first human to walk on Mars. Further explorations to Mars lead, late in 1973, to the discovery of a silicon coin close to the Sagan Canal and the excavation of an abandoned settlement. The discoveries proved the existence of life on other worlds and opened the debate of the earth having been colonised by Martians 10,500 years before.

Two years after the end of JFK's third and final term as US President in 1975 after an unprecedented period of world peace the United Nations elected JFK to the post of first World President.

His first task was to mediate in the Northern Ireland conflict. On one such diplomatic visit to Dublin he and his staff were killed when the helicopter in which they were flying crashed into the sea.

Kennedy was buried in Arlington Cemetery in a state funeral with full honours in Washington D.C. The whole nation held a week of mourning. At his grave, to symbolise his life's mission, an eternal flame of peace burns.

* * * * *

Jon stood before the shadow with the sword in his right hand. Out of the shadows it came, time's own nemesis. Ranulf sought retribution for a wasted life, revenge for injustice and payment for broken promises. Jon could see Ranulf's dark predatory eyes and he stepped into the dim light of the gateway, Ranulf looked him up and down and glared into Jon's frightened eyes.

"You're all going to die. You know that don't you ?" Ranulf said pointing accusingly at him, "All of you ! Cut down ! The ones you seek to free will never escape and you will never close my gateway !" And Ranulf laughed a mocking, cursing laugh that shook Jon's resolve.

Jon looked down at the sword in his hand. It felt snug and it reassured him. "Well, we all have to die some time." Jon said smiling, "Sooner or later it makes no difference. If fate has ordained it, I will die. Fortunately neither you nor anyone else will make any difference." They circled each other, staring each other out, waiting for one or other to make a move.

"You really haven't worked it out have you ?" Ranulf said sneering and spitting the words at him, "you and your pitiful friends have been used and have been made to fight a battle which isn't even yours. And evil will triumph once again ! You'll be cast like a stone to the next world - a world that only exists in your nightmares !"

Jon saw Ranulf was ready to attack and he lunged at Jon taking him by the throat, "pray that it exists, fool !!!!" And they fell to the ground.

* * * * *

Again the room began to become glow and Annelise could now see the sea of faces and the wandering souls. Something tugged at her sleeve, "Have you come to lead us back ?" It was a man in his mid thirties, his eyes were dark and his face pallid and grey.

"Yes, if you will come." she replied

"Will you take me back ?" The man asked, "I so want to see my Kathy again."

Behind her, in front of her, by her sides more hands clutching at her, touching her, grasping at her sleeve with wonder and questions. More and more they came until she was surrounded, the objects picked up and caressed as old friends held up to the now brightening light. She could hear a whisper that grew to a common voice, "Home. Home. Home. Going home", until it was a song of pure joy. Instinctively, she knew what to do and as she turned toward the gateway, they followed.

* * * * *

Ranulf sat on Jon's chest with both hands around his neck pushing the life out Jon's body.

Jon pushed with all the strength his will could summon and rolled over, grabbing the sword and gasping for breath.

Ranulf cursed Jon's tenacity, "damn you ! You only prolong your agony. Your final precious moments are slowly ticking away."

"Why do you do this Ranulf ?" Jon asked bent double, his hands on his knees, trying to catch his breath, "What pleasure do you get from it ? You live a hollow and empty life and the voices you hear are your own !"

"Whether mine or not they speak the truth to me ! Do not attempt to barb me with morality. I have had 400 years of mankind's hollow dreams !"

Ranulf was moving in on Jon again, waiting for the right moment and Jon raised the sword in defence, "What is it worth to have a clear conscience Ranulf ?"

And with that Ranulf rushed at him with a cry of revenge and with such ferocity that they were hurled into the gateway.

They landed on the cold of the Smithy's concrete floor. Realising Jon had had the wind pushed from him and was exposed Ranulf picked him up by the scruff of his neck and hurled him back through the gateway like a doll.

* * * * *

The Final Battle

Drew called again. Zetler was now slumped on the ground against the door frame and he seemed to struggle to look at his watch.

"Four and a half minutes. It's too long, we have only a few seconds left, " his voice was almost a whisper. Drew realised that there was something wrong and rushed over to Zetler who's energy seemed to be draining away like water from a breached dam. His face was grey, drawn and tired. Around them was an ominous silence.

Drew tried to move Zetler and placed an arm around his waist. He lifted but Zetler shook his head wearily wishing to stay where he was, "Drew. There is one explanation. One that I had not considered. It could be Jon and Annelise have no wish to return ! Perhaps everything they ever wanted was on the other side anyway !" Zetler eyes were filled with a stoic sadness.

Drew looked into Zetler's dimming eyes, "You mean they've gone ? For good?" Drew said shaking his head in desperation. Zetler nodded and then pushed Drew gently away. Drew looked down at the bodies of Jon and Annelise and he thought that they seemed to be glowing with a pale translucent blue light.

He looked back across to Zetler who had struggled to sit upright and was now sat with his legs crossed and hands on his knee as if ready to fall into a deep meditation.

Zetler looked up, his eyes were bright and full of energy and he smiled, "I have to return now. Until later, Drew my friend. Remember me..."

And with his work on earth at last accomplished he closed his eyes for the last time and his head bowed forward.

On the opposite wall of the Smithy Drew sat, helplessly as Zetler who had become his mentor and guru took on a soft blue glow in the twilight. It was a gentle radiance that started in his hands and head and heart and spread like a warm blue liquid coursing slowly through his now inert form.

It was as if Zetler had known of his destiny and had been patiently, "...*waiting for the moment but the moment has been waiting all the time.*."

He could only gaze in wonder and awe as the bright luminesence that shone like a beacon filled the room with a timeless light and energy and power and love. Light seemed to penetrate every dark recess and it spread skyward into the gathering night with a sharp precision of perfection. The power of love and energy of life enveloped and awakened him and revealed his thoughts of hope and vision. And he saw the truth of it.

* * * * *

Jon felt himself being lifted effortlessly and hurled like an unwanted toy across the room. His body landed in a crumpled heap and his side cried with the pain of impact. He dropped the sword and it rolled a few feet from his hand.

For a few seconds he lay motionless, gathering his strength and wits and trying to comprehend in his senselessness how he had arrived there. His foe seemed invincible with an unquenchable thirst for pain.

Then, out of the pain came a voice in his head, "reach ! For goodness sake reach !" The voice said urging him on.

Ranulf stood over him, his voice full of evil and victory. "So small, so easy," he muttered under his breath. He raised a hand and shouted his creed. "Another soul for your torment my Lord !"

Jon lay prostrate on the ground with a dark and menacing, evil shadow moving toward him. He was tired and had lost the will and strength to fight. He could only see the shadows before him and his life was fading.

"So near, too young, not ready, so much to do," he thought and could hear the end of all songs ringing in his ears .

Images of many lives flashed before him, images of life and death, of love and hatred, of birth and rebirth and of sleep and constant re-awakening.

"Get Up !" The voice said somewhere in his head.

He recognised the voice and knew what it meant. Something in his instincts knew what to do.

"Get Up !" The voice screamed at him again.

He focused on the power in the voice willing him to rise and he concentrated on it. Suddenly, with the combined force of the thousand tortured souls and the will to conquer and succeed he turned. Before him he saw the shadow's faltering steps, now unsure of victory and Jon rolled over to face him.

Jon snatched the sword from the ground and grasping it with two hands thrust it upward twisting the glittering steel blade into the shadow's body. Ranulf screamed in excruciating pain, with agony and bitterness as sorrow and anguish tortured his soul.

Jon crawled away from the dark shape of Ranulf who had now buckled to his knees. Jon fell back against the granite stonework exhausted.

Ranulf stared down in horror at the bright blooded blade that impaled his chest in horror. He felt no pain and was dumb struck in complete disbelief.

His eyes were staring wide with astonishment. Surely, this could not be his fate ? Then, dark shadows seemed to appear from stones themselves and they swept around him. They grasped at this body and began to tear it limb from limb. They shredded his soul like paper.

With a final desperate wail of anguish Ranulf began to fade.

"Help me ! Not this, no not this ! Anything but this !!!" He screamed. It was a pathetic cry that pleaded and as he clawed at the ground with his fingertips trying hold on.

"No ! Not this ! No further ! Please, mercy, help me, forgive me ! I was...I was only....Mercy ! No ! Please ! No !"

As the spirits claimed their prize Ranulf gave a final whimpering cry, "I am no more. I am oblivion....." And with a blinding flash of blue light the life force of Ranulf was gone.

Ranulf the stealer of spirits, had been destroyed and returned to earth reborn and redeemed for in those final moments Ranulf realised the true meaning of death and was purged of his sins.

And in the moment of rebirth he heard the voice of his angel. It was a voice of light. A voice of beauty. A voice of hope. A voice from one's most wonderful dream. A voice of love.

Calmly the it said :

"Ranulf. Be at peace. Somewhere in history you were wronged."

And the angel held Ranulf as a child in it's arms and said :

"And you could hate or hurt or kick or kill, you could shout or scream and fight or revolt, you could abhor or reject and despise or deride, you could condemn or judge and curse or cry, you could detest or disdain and, spite or slight, you could mock or scoff and spurn or sneer. And you could avenge..."

And the angel smiled and said, "....or you can love..."

Chapter 24

Rebirth

"And so the battle was won but the war continued. Evil would sometimes win a skirmish but never win the war, good always triumphant at the end and to the end ! For us all death and it's sleep come sooner or later. An eternity of heaven or hell, whichever has been ordained would await us. But, each day will surely come..."

Jarrat Toldon, Chronicles of the Future

"I don't believe in destiny or the guiding hand of fate,
I don't believe in forever or love as a mystical state,
I don't believe in the stars or the planets or angels watching from above,
But I believe there's a ghost of chance,
We can find someone to love, and make it last !"

Neil Peart

Drew lay on the cold floor of the Smithy, slumped against the dusty granite wall. He opened his eyes and rubbed his aching head. He felt exhausted and weary and his muscles ached. The Smithy was now lit by the dimming orange light of dusk and the cold glow of moonlight, it felt peaceful, safe and secure.

He had no way of knowing what the outcome had been but in his heart he felt they had been successful. He walked slowly over to the well and leaning on the side gazed over edge expecting to see the blackness and ripples of water, but right up to a few feet from the top it was filled with granite shards - the gateway had indeed been closed.

Of his friends and companions Jon, Annelise and Zetler there was no sign. By now they would be on the other side and he smiled feeling slightly envious. From his jacket pocket he took out the small flask which Jon had given him and unscrewed the silver top. The light was fading fast and he was beginning to feel a little cold. He walked outside to take a brisk lung full of night air and leaning against the oak door of the Smithy he raised the flask in salute to the stars with a hearty 'cheers' he took a mouthful of the aqua vitae. He felt the liquid run into his stomach and course through his body as a life's blood.

"Gees Jon," he said wiping his lips with his sleeve, "you're right ! It is better than bourbon !"

Drew felt at peace with the world. He had lost his friends but knew in his heart that they were in a better place than he. They had achieved their goals and were with the ones they loved.

He sat on the stone wall looking over the rape fields behind the Croft and watched as the skies darkened for night and the stars twinkled into life. In the North the first three evening stars winked liked diamonds. He smiled up at them and followed the band of the insubstantial Milky Way. He saw the billions upon billions of pin pricks, more than the grains of sand on a sea shore, stars that mankind through time had wondered at before him. He felt the warm glow of contentment. He knew his purpose. He was thrilled with the realisation that living was not all there was to life.

His spirits soared in euphoria as he planned his future. He felt his sorrows and cynicism lift like an ageless heavy burden and as he gazed on the bright glow of the Pleiades, he began to laugh and tears of joy began to well in his heart and he cried, not from pain or grief but from hope and happiness.

* * * * *

Around Annelise, where once was cold, sorrow and darkness were suddenly warmth, love and light. She stood in a large white marble hall almost like the nave of a great cathedral with a window on the world. Some distance away a man, that she did not at first recognise, lay on the ground comforted by a woman. Tens upon tens of souls walked through the light and were greeted by friends, family and loved ones, a young man by his wife and two daughters, another man by his brother, another by a lover.

Occasionally they would return to introduce her to a mother, a sister, a father, a brother, a friend and they would shake her hand, kiss her cheek and hug her tightly in thanks. She was surround by the warmth and joy of reunion. She didn't quite understand where she was or why she was there but could remember floating above the earth, a blinding flash of white light and then being enveloped by an blanket of love and warmth.

Then there was a voice behind her that struck a chord in her heart.

"Annelise ? Annelise ? It's me !" The voice said.

She turned to see Reinhardt and she fell into his arms.

"I love you Annelise," Reinhardt said stroking her hair.

"I know," she replied, "I know," and with his arm wrapped round her waist they walked toward the light.

* * * * *

As Jon lay on the ground he felt a hand on his shoulder and another stroking his head. It was a warm, loving hand, one very familiar to him. It was the touch it had dreamed of so often and missed so much. It was his wife's.

He opened his eyes and turned over. The pain seemed to have gone and the hall was now empty. They were alone. He sat up flinging his arms around his wife. They held each other tighter and closer than they had ever held each other.

"It's so good to see you again", he whispered "its been so long !"

"We never had a proper chance to say good-bye. It was so sudden. But, I was always there, listening to your every word. Helping where I could, giving strength when I was able."

"But, does this mean I'm...?", He asked.

"Yes Jon. You reached the other side. You've made it ! You're home !You've won !" As they embraced she said, "you seemed to have learnt so much in your time Jon. There are many people here who have waited to talk to you and thank you."

"When ? Now ?" He asked rising from the ground and putting his arm around his wife for support.

"No, no, later Jon. Come. Let's walk, we've some catching up to do ourselves."

"Has Daniel gone ?" He said knowing what the answer would be.

"Yes Jon. He had to go to his next earth time. But he sends his love and you will see him in the future."

Jon was warm and at peace. He looked over his shoulder and through a white framed window he could see the earth, a cloudy green and blue orb spinning in the darkness. Ahead of him he could see a bright white light warm and inviting. Jon looked back at the earth and stars twinkling around it and he held Ann close to him. "Love is eternal isn't it ?" He gazed into her bright green eyes and kissed her.

"Yes Jon" she smiled, "we are the lucky ones," and she looked into his deep brown eyes and they felt they were the only ones in the universe. They embraced, holding each other warmly and in the distance they heard a choir singing the sweetest 'Glorianna'.

* * * * *

Wilhelm Andreas Muhler had taken some convincing but had finally agreed that a week's holiday from the conservatory of music in Paris would be of benefit. He and his girlfriend had travelled from Paris on the train and already visited Wurzburg, Bonn, Munich and Salzburg and were now taking in the sights of Vienna. Their final stop of the day before an evening concert was at the newly opened Mozart mausoleum in St Stephen's Dom in the centre of Vienna.

After queuing for over half an hour they stood in front of the tomb. He touched the marble and read the inscriptions and epitaphs. He touched and felt the Austrian flag draped over the foot of the body. He remembered how the body had been found after being lost for two centuries. He looked again at the grand tomb, a fitting tribute to a great composer such as Mozart.

Overwhelmed by emotion something suddenly exploded inside him like a star burst, taking his breath away and telling him this was his destiny !

He knew he had talent but had never really thought he could be as successful as some of the great master composers. They had originally been ordinary men with extraordinary drive.

He could see himself conducting in the concert halls of the world. He could feel the adulation of his admirers. He could hear the wonderful music within him that he had long dreamed. He could taste that success about to come to him.

"Willie, are you ready ?" His girlfriend Kristal asked, "shall we go ?"

Wilhelm Andreas Muhler turned slowly to Kristal with a new fire in his eyes, nodded and said, "Yes ! Certainly ! Let's !"

On his return to Paris Muhler found a new vitality in composition and soon completed his Symphony No. 1 that was premiered later in the year. It was hailed as a masterpiece for one so young. His second symphony and first opera "Arthur and Guenivere" were glorious compositions and his fame spread across the globe.

Twelve months later he was engaged as the principal conductor for the Berlin Philharmonic following in the footsteps of Von Karajan and Bernstein. The pieces he composed as a boy and teenager were re-examined. They were recorded and performed by a wide cross section of the classical fraternity. In between his work in Berlin, he wrote his Piano Concerto No 1, a second opera and a piece of such simplicity it could be performed easily by children.

Muhler lived to his eighties and his vision and desire stayed with him to his death bed.

* * * * *

Reader. Let us take a final journey. Let us close our eyes and travel out toward the stars. Let us voyage past the moon and out toward the red planet of Mars with it's two moons high in the Martian sky.

As our feet touch the dusty earth we realise we can breathe quite normally.

We look over a red plane. In front of us a dried river bed snakes to the horizon. From the river toward the East is an intricate network of canals that if they were filled with water would irrigate the land.

We walk gently down to the valley floor onto a wide road that follows the line of one of the canals.

We realise that we are walking through a deserted and dead city. Soon we make out the shape buildings such as pyramids, temples, statues, high gateways, roads, palaces, buildings all hidden between the dust.

We stand in the outskirts of the capital city of the Western Martian Canton. It was laid waste in the wake of a comet that struck the plant three thousand years before utterly destroying the life on it. Out of a population of many billions there were only a handful survivors.

We stop in wonder at the foot of a large pyramid that dwarfs those of Egypt by ten times. Our eyes follow the sloping surface ever upwards and beyond the apex into the sky. It is a cold and wintry sky with the bright blue green star of our planet glinting back at us.

We gaze down at our feet and kick the cold red earth with our boots.

Something white, geometric, catches our eye in the dust and we kneel down to retrieve it.

It is flat and hexagonal and about an inch in diameter. It is light and feels slightly plastic. It is a small coin. It's six sides representing the six Cantons of Mars. It has a strange familiarity to it.

On the one side is a representation of the Pleiades cluster and on the other a strange symbol of ancient hieroglyphics representing its value. We hold it in the palm of our hand then between thumb and forefinger up to the dim light.

It is a small thing. It answers many questions and poses many more.

It proves we are not alone. It proves we are not who we think we are.

* * * * *

169

Rebirth

The mother has been in labour for some hours, she looks tired and drawn but bathed in sweat, she is, above all her pain, happy and content.

It had been a difficult birth and she is glad that it is over.

The small family are left to themselves.

By the window and looking out over the waving tree tops of poplars in the hospital grounds, the father holds his new born son and glows with pride.

He strokes the baby's blonde wispy hair. On its cheek, below its ear the baby has a tiny indentation - a birth mark. He kisses it on the forehead and it smells milky and clean.

The baby grips his father's finger in its tiny fist and in its silent secure slumber sighed and smiled. The baby feels warm, safe and secure born in to its new life.

The mother sits up, wincing in slight pain. "I've been thinking..." she says, picking up a baby card with a picture of a cartoon lion cub on it "...we could name him after a hero in the Bible."

Her husband smiled, "Sure. What do you have in mind ?"

"What about Daniel ?" She answered.

* * * * *

Afterword

No one leaves you
When you live in their heart and mind
And no one dies
They just move to the other side
When we're gone watch the world simply carry on
We live on laughing and in no pain
We'll stay and be happy
With those who loved us today

Steve Hogarth

Epilogue

"Hurry home to your heart, hurry home to the voice
There are times for inner changes, be ready for the choice
Hurry home said my love, hurry home to the stars
Start a new generation with a freedom that's ours."

Jon Anderson

o, like all stories, as this one ends the cycle of question and answer continues. With every new day lives begin and end in an unbroken spiral that revolves slowly through time.

How mankind has tried to slow time's inevitable journey.
Many have tried but all have failed.

We seem to cling on to this world thinking that death is the end.
But death it is just another beginning !
In this we should have hope, for in rebirth we have a chance to
learn the lessons we did not in this time.

For we must remember. No one is insignificant.
Fate charts a course that connects all our lives and our futures.
Each of us creates ripples that affect others.

It is left to us to live the best we can in hope, love and happiness.

To travel with joy and wonder along the long and unmapped roads.

To revel in our short times on this earth.

To learn the lessons our own souls need.

To write a few lines in history and to make a *difference*.

To crash and thunder like waves on the shores of time !

In this, and all your dreams, I wish you every success !

May You Be Heroes !

Rules for Being Human

1. You will receive a body. You may like it or hate it, but it will be yours for the entire period this time around.

2. You will learn lessons. You are enrolled in a full time school called life. Each day in this school you will have the opportunity to learn lessons. You may like the lessons or think them irrelevant and stupid.

3. There are no mistakes, only lessons. Growth is a process of trial and error and experimentation. The "failed" experiments are as much a part of the process as the experiment that ultimately "works"

4. A lesson is repeated until learnt. A lesson will be presented to you in various forms until you have learnt it. When you have learnt it, you can then go on to the next lesson.

5. Learning lessons does not end. There is no part of life that does not contain lessons. If you are alive, there are lessons to be learnt.

6. "There" is no better place than "here". When your "there" has become "here" you will simply obtain another "there" that will again, look better than "here".

7. Other are merely mirrors or you. You cannot love or hate something about another person unless it reflects in you something you love or hate about yourself.

8. What you make of life is up to you. You have all the tools and resources you need. What you do with them is up to you. The choice is yours.

9. Your answers lie inside you. The answers to life's questions lie inside you. All you need to do is look, listen and trust.

10. You will forget all this.

Author Unknown